# IT'S MAGIC!

## MICHAEL N. WILTON

# CONTENTS

1. How Was I to Know 1
2. The Best in the Business 15
3. Looking for an Answer 26
4. Going Undercover 35
5. Ripe for Plundering 48
6. His Own Ideas 57
7. A little Experiment 72
8. Watching as Instructed 85
9. What Body? 94
10. All He Wanted to Know 105
11. It Tells the Whole Story 121
12. Rebellion in the Ranks 133
13. Suitable for the Occasion 145
14. Doctor's Orders 160

*About the Author* 173

# 1

## HOW WAS I TO KNOW

'Don't take it too hard, chum,' sympathised the desk sergeant as Harry handed over his helmet, bringing an end to his short-lived career as a police constable. 'It wasn't me who gave you the push.' He lowered his voice in case he was overheard by his inspector. 'You weren't to know the fellow you tried to arrest in the dark was the new Chief Constable... and the fog an' all didn't help.'

Harry Bell heaved a sigh of resignation. 'Just my luck. If it was only that, I might have got away with it, after getting a right ticking off and a black mark on my records. I should have known better. It was arresting that blonde the next day for being drunk and disorderly that did it – how was I to know it was the mayor's wife.'

'Ah, well that's where you made your second mistake, son. It turned out to be his bit of crackling he was meeting on the sly – Saucy Sue, they call her. That wasn't your day, was it, when it all came out, especially as it happened to be his wedding anniversary. Never mind, my lad, that's all behind you now.'

'But what am I going to do?'

Catching sight of his inspector looming in the background, Sergeant Matthews hurriedly straightened up.

'Do? Why, buck your ideas up, young man and turn over a new leaf, that's what. Bear in mind what the force has been teaching you these past two years – discipline and dedication. Remember that, and you can't go far wrong.' He looked cautiously over his shoulder. 'Has he gone?' Putting the police helmet away out of sight, he relaxed visibly.

'Where was I? Oh yes. Now, how I see it is this. Forget about those... ahem, unfortunate lapses. Put it behind you and write it off as experience. You've got the rest of your life ahead of you.' He leaned over confidentially. 'Think of it as a new adventure. Take after your Uncle Ted – he wouldn't let any upset like that stop him getting where he is today, a respected and retired Detective Sergeant – it takes hard work and determination.'

'You should have heard what he said when I told him about it,' replied Harry despondently.

'Well, you'll just have to show him what you're made of.'

'Don't tell me, an idiot nephew without a job and no prospects, that's what.' Harry sighed. 'I owe the landlady for a week's rent, just to start with.'

Doing his best to cheer him up, the sergeant fished out a sheaf of 'wanted' notices and selected some at random. 'Hold your horses, you've still got a good brain and all that training to fall back on, don't forget. Why not have a go at one of these to keep you going. Look, there's a hefty reward for this one, if you catch him it would pay your rent for the next year or so.'

Harry took it with a sigh and read it. '"Butch Jones, real name unknown, escaped on remand, wanted for false identity and attempted murder. Armed, do not approach."' He handed it back. 'Urgh! Fat chance, he'll be miles away by now – that was six months ago.'

'Well, what about this one – "Scarface Willie on the run, convicted of assault and threatening witness."'

'Charming. He should be easy to find, with a name like that,' responded Harry drily.

'Oh, and there's this one that's just come in. "M. T. Banks, con artist and fraudster." Blimey, no wonder he took people in, his moniker was a dead giveaway.'

Harry scanned the details dubiously. 'The last one looks more promising. At least I don't need a gun with that character – just a lock-up safe, by the sound of it.'

'Have a go and keep in touch, lad. I don't usually get this feeling, but my instincts tell me you're someone worth watching with your background, so don't let me down. You're not the only one to find yourself in this position. There's plenty of others waiting their turn, so be prepared to give a hand when it's needed. Your Uncle Ted has a lot of faith in you, don't forget – he's a great mate of mine,' he ended gruffly. 'You can always give me a buzz if you need any back-up help, unofficially of course.'

'Thanks, Sarg,' Harry said. 'Don't think I don't appreciate it. I promise to follow up those tips. Meanwhile, I'll have a word with my landlady and see if she'll still have me.'

'Think nothing of it, Harry. Give my regards to Mrs M and don't forget...' he whispered, 'keep clear of that Chief Constable – Slaughter by name and by nature, they call him, with good reason.'

Without his familiar uniform to comfort and reassure him and attired in his old sport shirt and slacks, Harry felt almost undressed as he made his way out of the station for the last time, the desk sergeant's words of warning ringing in his ears.

He picked up his satchel from the cloakroom and was about to step outside when a hand descended on his shoulder and a familiar voice bellowed cheerfully in his ear, 'And where do you think you're going, my old china?'

He turned around, taken aback, and was confronted by his

fellow officer and old school chum, Freddie, backed by a row of grinning faces.

'You don't think we're going to let you go without a farewell knees-up, do you? Come on, the first round is on me, what d'you say, guys?'

To a chorus of cheers and slaps on the back, Harry found himself being steered in the direction of the nearest pub and a welcome pint was thrust in his hand to help him drown his sorrows.

'D'you know what?' appealed Freddie to the others. 'He was going to nip off without a word to anyone, the cheeky devil. This calls for a toast – to Harry Bell. May he forever be our friend and mate, wherever he goes and whatever the future holds for him. Cheers!' He followed this up with, 'Let's see 1969 goes out with a bang – here's to 1970 and good luck for better times to come.'

From then on events became a bit blurred, as far as Harry was concerned. So, when 'last drinks, gents' time was announced, Harry was barely conscious of being lifted off his stool and helped to Freddie's quarters for the night, wearing a blissful smile.

The next morning, by a supreme effort, he managed to stagger into the bathroom for a shower and a freshen up. Unable to face breakfast, and with the knowledge that his lodgings were a good eight miles away, he cursed himself for not accepting a lift from Freddie. But the thought of talking about recent events was too painful to bear, even with Freddie.

He had airily declined, offering the lame excuse that the exercise would do him good. To his relief, he covered the first few miles at a good pace with surprising ease, then coming across a signpost indicating that his destination, Tanfield, was still another five miles ahead, his optimism began to wane.

After taking a breather, he resumed his journey, resolutely putting aside his niggling aches, and after a while he became vaguely aware that he wasn't alone, despite the fact he was surrounded by miles and miles of bare hills and valleys, without a soul in sight. Pausing to get his second wind, he thought he heard a faint scuffling sound and looking around he caught sight of a scruffy, longhaired dog at his heels, looking lonely and slightly the worse for wear.

Bending down, he patted the animal, glad of an excuse to stop. 'Hello old boy, what are you doing in this part of the world?'

Unable to manage anything except for a muffled croak, the dog merely wagged his tail hopefully.

Assuming the animal must have strayed or, perish the thought, been dumped by some uncaring owner, Harry patted his head again reassuringly. 'Don't worry, we're nearly there,' he said pointing to the way ahead. 'Only a few miles to go.' He felt around the dog's collar for a possible clue to the animal's identity and was rewarded by the sight of a name plate. 'So that's what they call you, "Prince", eh? I shall have to bow before I speak to you in future, with a name like that.'

The dog managed another croak and looked up appealingly.

Remembering that he had passed a stream a short while back, Harry took pity at the state the dog was in, and picking him up, carried him back along the path and put him down at a handy bank, within easy reach of the water.

Wagging his tail feebly, the animal reached out a paw to steady himself and started to lick away happily, only to be rescued at the last minute when he nearly fell in. 'Steady on, old chap, take it easy. Mind you, it looks as if you could do with a bath. Feeling better now, are we?'

To his embarrassment, the dog started licking his fingers in gratitude. Carrying him back to the path to resume his journey, Harry patted him on the head encouragingly. 'There you are, old fellow – how do you feel. Off we go again, not far now.' It wasn't until they had gone a few yards that Harry could have sworn he heard the words, 'Thanks' being uttered. He paused in his tracks for a split second before carrying on automatically. *You idiot,* he told himself sternly, *it was only the wind you heard, you must have imagined it.*

He laughed at himself – it was not surprising he was feeling so light headed after the shock of parting company with all his mates after that last drinking session, despite all the orderly thinking his training had instilled in him.

The more he thought about it, the more absurd it all seemed, and he dismissed the idea, putting it down to tiredness, and instead focussed his mind on Mrs M, his landlady, and the thought of a relaxing and welcome cup of tea that would be waiting for him when he got back to his digs, and possibly crumpets, his favourite snack.

When he finally reached his destination he made for the reception area, secure in the knowledge he would be sure of a warm welcome. He pressed the bell on the counter, signalling he had arrived, and sat back anticipating all the familiar movements Mrs M usually made in the background – first, the kettle filling up, then the whistle of it coming to the boil and finally the delicious sound of tea being poured. As the minutes passed, however, in a deathly hush, he stirred restlessly and finally made the effort to get up, to discover for himself the reason for the unexpected delay.

At the sight of his landlady huddled over the table in the kitchen, her face buried in a handkerchief and sobbing her heart out, all thoughts of his own problems were instantly banished from his mind.

'Why, what on earth's the matter, Mrs M?' He tried to be practical, thinking of all the possible causes that would have left her in such a state. 'Is everything all right? Is someone ill or something... it's not... Sheila?' He forced the words out anxiously, thinking of her attractive daughter who occupied most of his thoughts.

'No, nothing like that – I'm only ruined, that's all.'

'Whatever is it?' He tried being jocular. 'The milkman hasn't eloped with that girl from the village – what was her name, Enid or something?'

'See for yourself.' She thrust a piece of paper at him. 'I'm up to my ears in debt, so my accountant tells me, that's what.' At the thought of the shame of it all, she burst into tears again.

'But that can't be right,' Harry protested loyally. 'Why, you've got a thriving business here. You're never short of lodgers and everyone knows you always pay on time. How can he make that out?'

'Then how come he says I've got to sell up to pay off all my debts – when I've never knowingly owed a penny in my life?'

'That's ridiculous,' said Harry scanning the figures. 'There must be a mistake. It says here you owe a small fortune – what does he expect you to do about it?'

'He wants me to hand the business over to him to pay off all my debts,' she exclaimed bitterly. 'I'm ruined.' She got up wearily. 'While you're having a look, I'll get your usual cuppa, dear.'

As he was absorbing the figures in sheer disbelief, she busied herself at the sink and handed over a cup of what looked like muddy liquid, forgetting in her anguish to add any milk and sugar.

Pushing it away gently, not wishing to add to her misery, Harry felt something lick his ankle and saw Prince looking up at him reproachfully. Sighing, Harry reached out for a packet of handy nibbles and tipped some into a bowl. 'Sorry, old lad. Help yourself.'

The dog regarded the offering mournfully and nosed it away somewhat disdainfully just as Mrs M handed over a plate of what Harry thought was scraps of leftovers.

'All I could find at short notice,' said Mrs M apologetically about the offering. 'I just can't think straight. Excuse me while I tidy myself up,' and throwing a handful of tissues in the nearest bin, she rushed off to the bathroom.

Making the most of her absence, Harry quickly put the burnt offerings down on the floor, hoping his new friend wouldn't notice.

The dog took one look at it, sniffed and gave Harry his second shock of the day. 'Call this food?'

Still recovering from his landlady's worries, Harry couldn't quite believe his ears. He'd put the previous weird experience down to tiredness, but twice in the same day was too much to accept. He held on to the table for support and blurted out the first thing that came into his head. 'Don't you like it, old boy?'

'Like it?' remarked the dog, indignantly. 'I wouldn't give it to the birds. By the way, don't call me 'old boy', if you don't mind. My name is Prince.'

'Of course, old...I mean, Prince,' he acknowledged feebly. He glanced round desperately, unable to think straight and trying to convince himself he wasn't going completely round the bend. Rallying, he tried to control his mounting hysteria. 'Look, I know it's not much, but I don't want to upset Mrs M. Can we talk about this elsewhere – like, in my room,' he found himself gabbling. 'Meanwhile, I'll see what I can find in the cupboard for you.'

Fighting off a strange legless feeling, he managed to get up and make his way to the food store where he knew Mrs M kept all her supplies and peered in furtively. 'Here we are, a jar of biscuits – will that do?'

'I suppose so, if there's nothing else going. I'm starving.'

'Here you are then, um Prince. Don't let Mrs M know,' he cautioned mechanically, 'they're her favourites.'

Between munching, the dog nodded obligingly. 'Don't worry – I'll keep mum.'

Wiping his forehead, Harry whispered, 'Here she comes. Don't forget.'

'Whatever must you be thinking of me,' apologised Mrs M, emerging from her room at last, looking distinctly ruffled. 'I was so upset about what that accountant went on about, I completely forgot about your tea. All I've got are a few sandwiches I was going to give him, and he never even bothered to look at them. Good riddance to him, that's what I say.'

'Don't give it another thought,' said Harry hastily. 'Sandwiches would be fine for us... I mean for me. I'm not very hungry – in fact, I'm feeling a bit worn out – it's been a long day after everything I've been through. I think I'll have an early night, if you don't mind,' he added, deciding it would be best to save news of his own situation until the morning, when she might be in a better state to take it in.

Before she could ask any more questions, he picked up a copy of her accounts with a sudden thought. 'Look, I know just the chap to put us in touch with someone who might know what it could all mean. Leave it to me, Mrs M. All I can say at this stage is, it doesn't seem right – I can't believe you owe all this money he's talking about.'

'Ooh, I'd be ever so grateful if you could, Mr Harry, I really would. I don't know how I'm going to tell Sheila – and the staff will have to go at this rate. It'll be a wrench. Whatever happens, I'll get a proper breakfast for you and I won't charge you any rent for a whole month, if you come up trumps. I just know it can't be right.'

'Don't worry, leave it to me,' repeated Harry, accepting the sandwiches gratefully. 'By the way, you don't mind if I have the dog in my room, do you? He's done his business, so he's perfectly respectful.'

'If you say so, Mr Harry,' she decided after catching sight of Prince. 'I don't usually allow dogs, but I'll make this a special case. Breakfast at the usual time then, good-night.'

After the door closed behind him, she looked at the clock reflectively. 'Funny time to go to bed, it's only six o'clock. Still, you never know with that police lot, they must be working him too hard, poor little devil.'

Once in the safety of his room, Harry collapsed in the nearest chair. Dabbing at his face, he laid the sandwiches at the dog's feet, finding he'd lost his appetite after the day's shattering events. 'Here you are, Prince old chap, help yourself.'

As he watched the dog tucking in, he did his best to work out what he was going to say that would help to make sense of the incongruous situation he found himself in. He tried out one or two opening remarks to himself, to see what it sounded like. *"Tell me old fellow, how long have you been able to talk like this?"* and *"Who taught you to speak?"* until all he could come up with weakly was, 'How did it happen?'

Pausing to take a breath after satisfying his immediate hunger, the dog looked up searchingly and put the question as if he was addressing a witness in court. 'Before I answer, will you swear that anything I tell you will not be repeated to anyone, at any time, outside these four walls?'

Comforted by the thought that nobody would believe him, even if he did, Harry replied feebly, 'I do.'

The dog nodded, as if satisfied, and replied darkly, 'All I can say is that if you did let it out, my head would be on the chopping block, and no mistake.'

'What are you talking about?' appealed Harry, completely mystified.

Ignoring his remark, the dog followed up with another question. 'Have you ever heard of a kingdom called "Palmesia"?'

'No,' said Harry with conviction, feeling rather like a school boy being put on the mat by his headmaster.

'That's where I come from – or came from,' the dog

corrected himself. 'After the revolution,' he added, as if that explained everything.

'What revolution?' asked Harry, feeling slightly bemused.

'Don't keep interrupting – you made me forget what I was going to say.'

'Sorry.'

'Now listen,' said the dog, settling down and making himself comfortable. 'This is where you might find it difficult to believe.'

It sounded like the understatement of the year. Past caring, Harry nodded obediently and tried to concentrate.

'It was like this,' said the dog getting into his stride. 'It was all set up for me to take over as the next in line, when this blasted cousin of mine decided he'd put a spanner in the works and collar the lot for himself. Are you with me?'

'Yes – at least, I think so,' said Harry cautiously, trying to keep up with him and hoping it wouldn't take too long to explain.

'Well, luckily my valet, Jazz found out what he was up to and tipped me off. But before we could do anything about it, that traitor of a cousin had gone and raised a rabble of an army and forced his way into the palace and took over.'

'What happened after that?' asked Harry bewildered. It was becoming too much for him to take in, and he found himself nodding off, despite the drama unfolding in front of him.

'What we didn't know was that old Jazz was a bit of a magician on the quiet, with powers nobody knew about, and guess what he did.'

'What was that?' asked Harry, feeling he was losing the thread of the conversation.

'He turned me into a dog, of course, so we could escape. Here, wake up – did you hear what I said?'

'Sorry... then why didn't he turn you back again, after you'd got away?'

'That's what I kept asking him. He said it was all part of the magic ritual and unless I did exactly what he told me, I'd find myself back where I was in the first place. I had to promise faithfully to follow the rules of the spell he used – I didn't have any option.'

'Ah,' said Harry, relieved to think that they seemed to be getting somewhere at last. 'What were those?'

'I wondered when you were going to ask me that. He said I'd have to carry out some sort of programme of helping others before he could use his spell to put it all right again. If I breathed a word about what happened to anyone, I might as well forget about the whole exercise – and I wasn't to contact him about it, unless it was urgent.'

'What kind of help do you think he meant?' asked Harry, glancing hopefully at his bed.

'He said I'd know when I've done it,' answered Prince, nudging him hopefully. 'You have any ideas?'

But Harry found he could no longer think up an adequate answer that would make sense after such an extraordinary story. Exhausted by the shattering events of the day and the recent astonishing revelations, all he could do was reach out and seek the comfort of his bed, and as soon as his head touched the pillow he was lost to the world.


Turning over restlessly in bed in the small hours, Harry woke up and tried to get to sleep again, but all he could think about was Prince's extraordinary tale. How could anyone in his right mind, especially a Prince – if he was to be believed – allow himself to get into such a situation, without being able to do anything about it. It didn't make sense.

Drowsily, he thought back to his own family history that Uncle Ted was fond of relating when he'd had too many drinks after a Saturday night out, and began to see a parallel of some sort emerging. What if that old wives' tale about Grandad's past was true after all, and he himself was a distant relative of an earl, even if he was not likely to be ever recognised as such given the circumstances.

He'd looked up pictures of the old boy in the family album whenever he had time and his grandad had been strikingly handsome, and no doubt attracted attention from a number of female admirers, even though he was only a butler when the picture was taken. According to the family records, he was always on the lookout for a more adventurous life and at the first opportunity volunteered for active service overseas to escape domestic duties. His bravery in battle soon marked him out and after gaining his stripes, he was promoted from the ranks to an officer and awarded a medal for gallantry, and that was probably how he caught the eye of the Earl's daughter, Lady Mary, when he was home on leave, resplendent in his uniform. Unfortunately, having served the family as a butler, their blossoming romance was not regarded at all favourably by the Earl, and when Lady Mary fell pregnant the whole affair was hushed up and his grandad was shown the door.

To safeguard the family's reputation, the Earl persuaded his daughter to marry a distant cousin called Percy to keep it in the family and hopefully avoid any scandal. Then it all came to an end when Lady Mary died in childbirth, and his grandad was left with no claim on the estate. Although he eventually married and settled down, it was said that he never got over his first love and later died of a broken heart.

All this came to light when Harry discovered a bundle of letters in a desk drawer one day, written by his grandad at the time he tried to gain access to his baby son, without success.

It was a secret romance and remained secret, and one that Harry's father carried to his grave, for despite his repeated requests, the Earl ignored his entreaties and refused to recognise him; and his son, the present Earl, carried on the tradition.

*Uncle Ted was left with the responsibility of bringing me up and paying for my education,* reflected Harry as he turned over in bed, seeking a more comfortable position. *He refused to take any credit for it. Not only that, he encouraged me to join the police force as a cadet, and a fat lot of good it did him. All I did was to muck the whole thing up by being sacked, so how can I ever repay him?* He would never be in a position to propose to Sheila at this rate even if they did say that 1970 was to be a year of opportunities. *Fat chance.*

Then he remembered the comforting things his desk sergeant had said about facing up to challenges and by helping others, and the last thought that crossed his mind as he dozed off was... *Don't forget about those accounts...*

## 2

## THE BEST IN THE BUSINESS

The next morning, it was the insistent knocking on the door, followed by his landlady's familiar voice, that woke him up.

'Breakfast in ten minutes, Mr. Harry.'

'Right-Ho,' he mumbled, turning over and rubbing the sleep from his eyes. As he did so, last night's events started flooding back, making him wince at the memory. He peered over the side to see if the object of his thoughts was still there.

The sight of Prince spread out happily on the carpet convinced him that he hadn't dreamed it all and reminded him of the problem that confronted him, and one he had to try to solve, if he was to remain sane.

What on earth was he going to do about it? The recollection of what Prince had told him was so bizarre he still couldn't take it in. All that talk about his valet being a magician and turning him into a dog left an awful lot of questions to be answered, before it could even begin to make sense. For instance, where was that blighter of a valet he was talking about while all this was going on, and why didn't he turn up when Prince started following him home yesterday?

He scratched his head and finally gave up. His more immediate problem was how he was going to help Mrs M get out of
the awful mess she was in, before he decided what to do about
himself; and that meant finding someone to check those
accounts to get at the truth. His mate Freddie was bound to
know – his knowledge of useful contacts was a by word
amongst all their friends, or was before he got the chop, he
admitted ruefully. Meanwhile, what was he to do about
the dog?

The thought of leaving Prince behind when he might come
out with some rash remark in an unguarded moment, sure to
upset Mrs M, made him go hot and cold all over. It would be
enough to send her over the edge and end up with her getting
herself carted off to the loony bin, as if she didn't have enough
to worry about already. In the short time he had got to know
her, she had become more like a motherly aunt than a landlady,
in the same league as his Uncle Ted.

No, his only solution was to take Prince with him and find
something for him to do that wouldn't ring any alarm bells
while he was following up the mystery about the accounts. A
sudden thought struck him.

*Of course, after being thick as thieves with that magician valet,
he might come up with a trick or two that we haven't thought about,
that might solve everything,* he reminded himself optimistically.
His mind settled, he dressed in double quick time and waking
up Prince, led him into the kitchen.

'Ah, there you are, dear,' greeted Mrs M. 'Get stuck into that
lot and you won't come to no harm. I've rustled up something
for that dog of yours as well. Sit yourself down. Oh, by the way,
I've made a copy of those dratted accounts, so you can hang on
to them as long as you like, no hurry as far as I'm concerned.'

'Thanks, I was just wondering about those,' confessed
Harry, relieved to see that a bowl had been set aside for Prince,
full of tasty treats. He added casually, anxious not to spoil her

present mood, 'When are you expecting that accountant to come back, did he say?'

'I told him I'd think about his mouldy offer, and he had the cheek to invite me to go to that village 'do' with him tonight while I made up my mind, as if I would,' she said indignantly. 'Now you're looking into it, he can blessed well wait, the worm – he didn't give me any warning about the accounts getting in the state they're in, so why should I?'

'Quite right,' agreed Harry, pleased to see she was adopting the right spirit. Pushing his plate away at last with an effort, he grinned his appreciation. 'That was a feast, Mrs M. I won't want anything more until supper. Now, if you'll excuse me,' he said as he made for the phone, 'I'll give my friend Freddie a buzz and see if he can help.'

'While you're doing that I'll go and give Sheila a shout. Poor duck, she was all set up about going to that village do herself tonight. That dreadful news of mine has probably put the dampers on it.'

'Don't worry. Knowing Sheila, they'll be queuing up to take her, especially her boyfriend,' said Harry enviously, wishing he was in a position to ask her himself.

Putting aside his cherished hopes, he broke off as Freddie answered. 'Hi, Freddie, have you got a minute?' and in a few short sentences explained what he wanted. 'You know some-one, great. Look, I wonder if you could do me a favour. I need to see him asap, but I haven't got any transport. You will? That's brilliant. In ten minutes? Right away, even better. Look forward to seeing you.' Catching sight of his landlady's anxious face, he added reassuringly, 'That's all fixed, he's off duty. Come on, Prince, it's time we were off.' Slipping on his jacket, he picked up a copy of the accounts and turned to go. 'Must dash. Oh, and don't worry about Sheila,' he said awkwardly, 'I'm sure she'll be all right. Bye.'

'Thanks ever so, Mr Harry.' Mrs M waved him off. 'Hear

that, ducky,' she called up the stairs, 'Harry says no need to worry about the dance, he'll sort something out for you.'

Sitting back comfortably as he adjusted his seat belt, feeling they seemed to be getting somewhere at last, Harry enquired, 'He's good, is he, this chap, Morrison, the one you were talking about?'

'None better,' assured Freddie, putting his foot down on the pedal. 'With a bit of luck, we'll catch him before he goes off duty. Not that he's on a regular beat,' he explained, 'he's one of the backroom boys at HQ. He'll tell you all about it when we see him. Now, what are you up to these days? Doing a bit of freelancing on your own, are you?' He chuckled. 'I hear you tried to arrest our dear old Chief – I'd love to have been there and seen his face when it happened.'

'You wouldn't have,' Harry assured him. 'He wasn't very amused.' He paused, trying to summarise his recent experiences. 'It's about my landlady, she's in a spot of trouble.'

'Not your Mrs M – I don't believe it. She's one of the straightest old birds I've ever met.'

'That's what we all thought, until her accountant turned up. According to these figures,' he held up the piece of paper he was holding for his friend to see, 'she's up to her neck in debt. I don't believe it for a minute, and I need someone to explain what's behind it.'

His friend whistled. 'Well, if anyone can, I put my money on old Morrison. He's the best in the business.' He slowed and turned through the gates ahead. 'Here we are. I'll leave you to it, he knows why you're coming. I'll have a quiet fag while I wait. He's on the second floor, room eight. Best of luck.'

Morrison, he was informed grudgingly at the desk, could spare a few minutes to see him, as long as it didn't take too long. Put off somewhat by the rebuff, Harry hurriedly revised what he was going to say in the time he had available as he was being ushered in.

To his surprise, the superintendent welcomed him cordially and waved him to a chair. 'Sorry to ask you to keep it brief – I'm up to my eyes in it as usual, I'm afraid, as you can see by my in-tray. Now what's all this that young Freddie has been telling me? I hear your landlady is in a spot of trouble.'

Relieved at the warmth of his reception, Harry began to relax and handed over his copy of the accounts while he explained what had happened.

Seeing the accounts, the superintendent made some room on his desk and started to study the items. 'Hmm, d'you think this accountant knows what he's doing? Why has he left it so long to tell her he's left her overdrawn, adding up to a tidy sum by the looks of it.'

At his words, Prince sat up and started whining, and his actions caught the superintendent's attention. 'I say, don't look now, but that pooch of yours is trying to tell us something. Does he want to go wee-wees?'

'No, no,' said Harry quickly. 'He's fine.'

A puzzled expression appeared on the other's face. 'That's funny, for a moment, I thought he was trying to write some-thing on that scrap of paper I dropped just now – must get my eyes tested.' He adjusted his spectacles with a laugh and dismissed the idea.

'Nothing like that,' Harry assured him hurriedly. 'He's probably a bit peckish – he gets like that sometimes.' He reached down, pretending to pat the dog while he scanned the message. Written as it was with a dog's paw, using a pencil that had lain on the carpet under the desk, it was almost illegible, but he managed to decipher it. It read, *"Tell him about the offer."*

Catching on, Harry quickly crumpled up the paper and hurriedly changed the subject. 'I forgot to mention. The accountant also said he was prepared to cancel the debt if she agreed to hand over the business to him, the cheeky blighter.'

'Did he, by Jove,' the superintendent said thoughtfully. 'That's interesting – puts an entirely different complexion on the matter.' He got up reluctantly. 'Sorry, I can't promise to give you an answer right away, but I'll take those accounts home with me tonight, seeing it's urgent, and hope to get you an answer as soon as I can.'

As his visitors left, he stroked his chin pensively, 'That's damned odd – I could have sworn that dog was trying to write something.' He shook his head. 'That'll teach me not to have that extra scotch so soon after lunch.'

Relieved to know he was in good hands, Harry left the room, and as he was shown out by one of the officers he thought the man's face looked vaguely familiar, probably someone he'd seen when visiting the sergeant, he thought. Looking at his watch he realised that Freddie had given up waiting so he called a cab. By the time he got back to his lodgings the incident with the police officer had slipped his mind and he was jolted out of his complacency by a fresh problem.

As he was about to knock on the door, it was opened by Mrs M who had been looking out for him and pulled him inside with a whispered, 'Shush, come into the kitchen.' Shutting the door behind them, she brushed aside his explanations. 'Never mind about the accounts for a moment – it's about Sheila.'

Thinking he was about to hear something dreadful, Harry nerved himself up. 'She's not been in an accident, has she?'

'No, nothing like that. It's that boyfriend of hers, Arnold. D'you know what he's done?'

Before he could hazard a guess, she wailed, 'He's gone and broken off their engagement, that's what, and you know why?'

Ignoring his sudden lifting of spirits, she hissed contemptuously, 'Because he found out about that blasted accountant and his report, that's what – and he's gone and dumped her, the swine. Now that the word's got around, nobody is likely to ask her out.'

She dabbed her eyes mournfully. 'What she wants is someone she can rely on with a good steady job, somebody she can trust.' She brightened. 'Then I thought of you.'

As her words sank in, Harry swallowed. 'Steady on, Mrs M.' He braced himself. 'I think I ought to tell you...'

'But you must, Mr Harry,' she insisted, 'you promised to help.'

'I know I did,' he admitted reluctantly, 'but the truth is, I'm out of a job.' Before she could stop him, the whole story came out in a rush. 'So you see, I'm not much in a position to help her.'

'Oh dear,' was all she could say as the tale came to an end. 'What are we going to tell Sheila – you said you'd fix it.'

'I know, and I meant it at the time – I didn't think that Arnold of hers was going to behave in that underhand way. I can hardly ask her myself – she's had enough shocks for one day.'

'I know,' said Mrs M brightly, inspired by a sudden thought, 'why don't we tell her you're working under cover for the police, checking up on my accountant. He told me he was going to the village do, so it would be a perfect excuse.'

Attracted for a moment by the thought, Harry considered the proposal doubtfully. 'But I'm not in the police any more, and besides, what if we bump into someone I know?'

'That's not likely – it's only the local village do. Come on, you'd enjoy yourself, and it would give Sheila something to look forward to.'

Much to his surprise, Sheila was delighted at the offer when it was put to her – particularly when she realised it would be an ideal opportunity to spy on that wretched accountant who had somehow got her mother's accounts into the awful state they were in, and landed them right in the soup. At the same time, it would give her the chance to get her own back on that so-and-so of a boyfriend of hers, if she saw him.

As a result, she put a special effort into making herself presentable, with such a stunning effect Harry was left speechless in admiration.

'Will I do?' she asked nervously when the time came to leave, doing a little twirl to see if he approved.

He gulped and offered his arm. 'You'll be the belle of the ball,' he assured her.

It was only a short walk to the Town Hall where the event was being staged, and every step had a magical quality of its own in Harry's mind. He never thought he would have the nerve to invite her, given his circumstances – and to end up being virtually begged by Mrs M to escort her was icing on the cake as far as he was concerned.

Determined to make the evening a success, he made sure he had enough cash left in his pocket before they started so she could enjoy herself, and leave him enough to pay for drinks and a sit down whenever he thought she'd had enough. But as the evening wore on, Sheila seemed to have thrown off her earlier mood of depression and became more animated by the minute – to such an extent that some of the other dancers decided to leave the floor to watch them as they became the increasing focus of attention and interest.

In the end, Sheila got so flushed and a little exhausted by it all that Harry thought it was time to call a halt and gently steered her towards their table and ordered drinks.

'Oh, thank you Harry, that was wonderful. I could have danced all night.'

'Your previous partner wasn't so interested in dancing then, I take it?' he asked tactfully.

'*Arnold*, don't remind me.' She gulped down a mouthful, as

if to erase the memory. 'I thought I trusted him, the so-and-so. Not like you, Harry. Mummy told me about your efforts to sort out those accounts – is there anything I can do to help?'

Harry leaned forward cautiously. 'As a matter of fact, you could start by pointing her accountant out to me, if you could – I've never met him myself. Your mother did say he was planning to be here tonight.'

Sheila giggled. 'Don't look now, but he's sitting just a couple of rows behind us, with some tart he's picked up from somewhere. What a sight she looks – I don't know where he digs them up.' She reached out and patted his hand. 'I'm so lucky. She's not the only one, I'm told. And he's just as bad. I don't know why Mummy took him on in the first place. With a name like he's got, I ask you – "Reginald Adrian Trustworthy",' she said scornfully. 'I'm surprised that anyone would *think* about taking him on. It spells rat, if you think about it, and that's what he is. I never could trust him, not like you. Oh Harry, I'm having such a wonderful time, thanks to you – I could kiss you.' Suiting action to words, she darted around the table and planted a big kiss on his cheek.

Feeling the sudden warmth of her body, Harry completely forgot himself and took her in his arms and returned her kiss with interest.

Breaking free with a gasp, Sheila gazed up appealingly. 'You wouldn't ever let me down, would you, Harry? I couldn't bear it, after all I've been through lately.'

Tilting her face up, Harry said simply, 'I wouldn't dream of it. I think I fell in love with you the first moment I saw you.'

'Oh, Harry,' she said breathlessly. 'I can't believe this is happening.' She fanned her face. 'I feel so hot and sticky all of a sudden, I must go and freshen up, if you'll forgive me, darling. I shan't be long, promise. That reminds me, while I'm gone, have a quick peep in this thing to see what that man looks like, so they don't notice what you're doing.' She rummaged in her handbag and fished out a small hand mirror.

Left to himself, Harry sat there with an ecstatic expression, staring dreamily into the distance, totally oblivious of his surroundings, quite content to go on dreaming.

Distracted after a while by the sound of the dance band striking up again, he was vaguely aware of holding something in his hand and held it up to peer at it in a disinterested sort of way, out of curiosity.

What he saw in the reflection made him sit up suddenly with a startled cry and the mirror flew out of his hand and lay shattered on the floor in a thousand pieces.

Attracted by the commotion, the young lady in question tiptoed up behind him to discover what all the fuss was about. Seeing him, she uttered a cry of delight and swooped on him, flinging her arms around his neck. 'Oh Harry, it's me, Sue. I've been looking for you everywhere. If it hadn't been for you, I'd never have found out what an awful man that mayor was. He promised to marry me and all the time he had a string of call girls I never knew anything about. If you hadn't tried to arrest me, I would never have guessed. How can I thank you.' Before he could protest, she began to smother him with kisses, just as Sheila emerged from the Ladies room and witnessed the event.

'*Oh, Harry – how could you!*'

Pulling himself free with an effort, Harry tried to wipe off the smudged lipstick and explain at the same time defensively. 'Wait, Sheila darling – it's not what you think. I – er helped this young lady once when I made the mistake of trying to arrest her...'

Before he could say any more, she snatched at a menu the waiter was holding out and threw it at him.

'I know all about that little tramp. If that's what they do every time you try to arrest someone,' she sobbed before storming off, 'you can keep your "Saucy Sue" and get lost, as far as I'm concerned.'

Reeling from the onslaught, Harry attempted to follow her in the vain hope that nobody had overheard the exchange, as the band in the background tried to drown her departing words. Unhappily for one man, furtively hiding himself behind a newspaper in the corner, the words struck home. Making for the nearest phone, he made an urgent appointment to see his PR adviser. 'Tell him it's Mayor Fox calling,' he hissed. 'Yes, first thing tomorrow.' Wiping his forehead, he sat back nervously, before reaching out for his bill.

# 3

## LOOKING FOR AN ANSWER

Turning over in his mind the shattering events that had occurred, Harry searched hopelessly for an answer as he trudged back to his lodgings. One thing was abundantly clear. After the latest fiasco, he hadn't got a hope in hell of getting Sheila to forget what had happened – particularly so soon after being let down by her former boyfriend. Plunged in gloom, he paused before entering, debating what was the best thing to do.

Before he could make up his mind the decision was made for him by a furious outbreak of barking from Prince, who he had left locked up inside his room.

The noise woke Mrs M who appeared at the door, peering out. 'Whatever is the matter?' she asked fearfully. 'Oh, it's you, Mr Harry. What's going on? First Sheila comes storming in without a word and goes straight up to her room, and now you turn up, looking like a shipwreck waiting to happen. Come and sit down and tell me all about it. On second thoughts, you'd better let that dog out to do his wee-wees before there's an accident. While you're doing that, I'll make us a cup of cocoa to help calm us down.'

Harry did as he was bid, relieved to know he had a few

moments to think up what to tell Mrs M, knowing how much she doted on her daughter. Prince, on the other hand, was not content to wait. As soon as they were out of earshot and he had relieved himself, he looked up eagerly. 'Well, how did it go? You're home early. Tell me all about it.'

Knowing he wouldn't get any peace until he did, Harry heaved a sigh and embarked on the whole unhappy episode, adding a few background details to explain what led up to it.

Chewing it over, Prince piped up thoughtfully, 'Gosh, I don't remember anything like that happening to me– some people have all the luck.'

'Call that luck?' said Harry despondently. 'She'll never forgive me after that.'

Hearing a call from inside, Prince gave his verdict. 'Now's your chance to find out.' He added, 'Looks like it's time to get back and face the music.'

Turning, Harry agreed reluctantly. 'Come on then. I'll have to be careful what I say though.'

He shuddered. 'She doesn't know anything about that Sue episode, so don't butt in and give the game away.'


Once inside and soothed by a welcome cup of cocoa, Harry found himself describing their evening out, presenting it in a suitably modified form that he hoped would be more accept-able. However, his explanation was cut short by Mrs M who wanted to know if they had seen the accountant and whether they had discovered anything. Impatient at the lack of news, she stirred restlessly and was on the point of going upstairs to question Sheila further on the subject when Harry managed to restrain her.

'I shouldn't worry her just now, Mrs M. I think the dancing tired her out,' he said diplomatically. To divert her attention, he switched to the subject most dear to her. 'Did I tell you that the

Superintendent I saw promised to take those accounts home with him, so he could check them over. Leave it with me. I'll get in touch with him first thing tomorrow morning to see if he has come up with anything.'

Brightening up at the news, Mrs M pressed his arm gratefully. 'If you would, Mr Harry, it would take a great load off my mind. I've been so worried about it all, I think I'll follow Sheila's example and have an early night. Breakfast at the usual time?'

Harry thought quickly. 'No, don't worry about me, Mrs M. I'll grab something before I go. You make sure you have a good night's sleep and see to it that Sheila does, as well. Meanwhile, I've got to ring my friend Freddie and find out if I can cadge a lift first thing in the morning to see about those accounts, before he goes on duty.'

'All right, I'll leave it to you,' she agreed and gathered up her things to go. 'I'm too tired to argue about it, after all I've been through.'


'Looks as if you've got away with it,' confirmed Prince, as the door closed behind her.

'Let's hope she feels a bit better tomorrow,' sighed Harry. 'Meanwhile, I'll see if I can get hold of Freddie.'

His luck was in, but it would mean an early start so he made a mental note to get up in time to let Prince out and avoid disturbing the others. Luckily his training as a police cadet made it easier, enabling him to grab a quick bite and slip Prince out for a quick wee before Freddie arrived.

As soon they exchanged greetings and got underway, Freddie broke the silence. 'I say, I've been thinking about those figures you mentioned. What sort of period are we talking about – would they be quarterly or annual, do you think?'

Harry reflected. 'I don't know. I suppose those accounts

would tell us – of course it would depend on when Mrs M took him on.'

'If it was annual, you'd think he would have had the sense to tell her about it before now, instead of leaving it this late. Sounds a bit odd to me.'

Harry was about to agree, when to his horror a familiar voice joined in from the back seat.

'Sounds downright fishy to me.'

The sudden interruption out of the blue caused Freddie to swerve, and Harry shut his eyes waiting for the inevitable crash. By a miracle, they managed to avoid colliding with an oncoming lorry, before Freddie got his voice back.

'I say,' he gulped. 'That was damned clever. How did you manage to do that, without moving your lips?'

Harry waved a hand at the back seat in an attempt to shut Prince up, before assuming a suitably modest expression. 'Just a knack, I suppose. I was taught by some Johnny at the last police concert I helped with,' he invented on the spur of the moment. 'He was an amazing ventriloquist.'

'He must have been,' agreed Freddie. 'I say, what a wheeze. You could earn a small fortune doing that. It would save you starting up that private eye lark you were telling me about.'

'I think I'll wait until I find out what the Superintendent comes up with first,' said Harry hastily.

'I know, but that was amazing. You could always fall back on that, if you ever change your mind.'

'Quite. Er, do you know, I believe we're nearly there. Do you mind waiting while I try to see if Morrison's free?'

'Of course,' agreed Freddie. 'I'm not on duty for a while. Besides, I want to hear you doing that ventriloquist act again, before I go. It was brilliant.'

'I couldn't promise anything,' protested Harry hurriedly. 'It's just a knack of mine I picked up. It comes and goes,' he said, casting a warning glance at the back seat.

'Don't worry about your dog,' reassured his friend. 'He'll be all right with me – it will give me someone to talk to, while you're in there.'

Harry swallowed. 'No, if you don't mind, I'd better take him with me. It's time he did his wee-wees.'

Bundling Prince out of the back seat and clipping on his lead, Harry made his escape.

Luckily, he managed to get in to see the Superintendent before the latter started to work on his in-tray. Waving Harry towards a seat, he opened his briefcase and spread Mrs M's accounts out on the desk in front of him.

'That was a pretty little puzzle you set me yesterday. I've been going over it so many times, my wife told me I wouldn't get any supper unless I gave it a rest and packed it in for the night.'

Apologising for the trouble he was giving, Harry ventured. 'I'm sorry – so it was a waste of your time?'

The Superintendent rubbed his chin. 'No, not by all means – I like a challenge. Tell me though, how many people would you say stayed at this lodging place of yours, on average?'

Taken aback at the request, Harry cast his mind back. 'Bit difficult to say, offhand. It varies according to the time of the year – anything from one or two at the slack times, to a dozen or so in the racing or football season, for instance. Now that word has got around about the state of the accounts though, they've all been finding excuses to find somewhere else to stay.'

'That's interesting.' The other turned over the pages as he absorbed the information. 'Looking at some of the details of these accounts, for instance, I get the impression that your lodging place is more like a hotel, going by the size of the orders involved.' He mused, 'It's almost as if...'

'...he's lifted the figures from someone else's account.'

'It's funny you should say that,' said the Superintendent, mishearing the source of the interruption. 'That's the same thought that passed through my mind.' Then as the sound of the voice sank in, he looked up startled. 'That's funny, I thought for a moment it was your dog talking – silly me. Perhaps my wife was right, I've been working too hard lately.'

'People often get that impression,' broke in Harry hurriedly. 'It's because he sits so close to me usually.'

He took a deep breath. 'If we are right,' he followed up the train of thought, 'it's as if he's somehow using figures from something much larger, like a hotel account... and the only one around here that fits the bill would be the one owned by the mayor himself, Alderman Fox.' They looked at each other, struck by the same coincidence.

'That's nonsense of course,' remarked the Super. 'I can't imagine that a figure of his standing would think of getting his accounts mixed up with a small rental place like this. That accountant's no fool, why would he get involved in a shady operation like that. He'd never live it down, stands to reason.'

'And if there were a shadow of truth in it,' began Harry slowly, 'how on earth could anyone begin to prove it?'

'You've said a mouthful,' agreed the Super. 'He's not likely to admit it, even if it were true. Those figures can only mean one thing – whoever it was, he must have been up to his ears in debt.'

'I wonder, by any chance,' suggested Harry, still musing on the possible connection, 'if the mayor uses the same accountant?'

'I'm afraid I can't help you there,' said the Superintendent, 'different county.' He passed back the accounts reluctantly. 'I dare say your Mrs M could lodge a complaint if there's anything in it, but it would take some time, and meanwhile I expect she's losing most of her customers on the strength of it.'

'And she can't afford to give me free board and lodgings while this is going on,' finished Harry, coming to a decision. 'I think I'll have a word with my old sergeant; he did say he'd help me if I ran into a spot of trouble. Anyway, it was good of you to run your eye over these accounts. Let me know how much I owe you.'

'Think nothing of it,' assured the other, getting up and shaking hands. 'Your uncle is an old mate of mine. Give him my regards when you see him.'

Emerging with Prince in tow, Harry quickly explained the situation to Freddie.

Hiding his disappointment that there would be no time for any more ventriloquist acts, his friend opened the door with a flourish. 'Hop in, the "Freddie taxi service" awaits your bidding. Desk sergeant, here we come. Tell you what, while you're having your chat with the sergeant, I'll grab a snack in the canteen and get them to put something by for you. When you've finished, you can join me and we'll toddle off home together. That's no problem, I only live down the road from you, anyway. If anyone at the station wants to know why,' he grinned, 'I'll say I came over all faint, because you wouldn't do that ventriloquist act you promised. Only joking,' he added cheekily.


'It's funny you should ask me that,' commented Sergeant Matthews, as Harry's tale about the accounts finally came to an end. 'I know of a job that's come up that might help you solve your problem – and it would help us out at the same time.' Seeing Harry's puzzled expression, he fished out a report. 'Here, take a look at this.' He thumbed through the pages. 'It's an outfit called Executive Services. We've had our eyes on them for some time and my instinct tells me they're up to no good. We had one of our plain clothes chaps check them out after a number of characters we know mysteriously disappeared, just as we were about to nab them.'

'What do they do, and how would that help me?'

The desk sergeant pointed to the description. 'As you see, they provide a public relations advice service for senior executives. Put simply, their job, according to our lads, is to cover up anything the clients wouldn't want the public to know about.'

He added heavily, 'And the vacancy in question is to replace one of their PR men who disappeared at the same time as one of the characters we wanted to arrest.'

Anticipating his next question, the desk sergeant came to the point. 'Just between you and me, we've heard that your accountant friend is heavily involved with this outfit and their activities. What we want is someone to work there undercover and find out exactly what they are up to, and this is where you come in.

'They could be behind a number of cases we've never been able to prove – anything from blackmail and robbery to one or two unexplained deaths.' He raised a hand reassuringly. 'We don't want you to do anything that would get you into any trouble. You just need to let us know, from time to time, what the devil is going on, so we can decide what to do.' He added as an inducement, 'You will no doubt be interested to learn that one of their top clients is our own mayor, Alderman Fox.'

'But,' Harry protested, 'how can I work under cover? The mayor will remember me from when I tried to arrest his girlfriend for being drunk and disorderly.'

His objection was waved aside. 'Don't worry about that, we'll fit you up with a new identity. I know, you can call yourself Tom Smith, for instance. Nobody will be able to check on you with a name like that. We'll fill in the application form and send it off on your behalf. Meanwhile, now you're seconded, you can claim expenses.' He got up and handed over some notes from a drawer. 'This should keep Mrs M happy for the time being. Let me know when you hear from them. I expect they'll want to interview applicants pretty quickly given the hole they're in, according to rumours.'

'Thanks, Sarg.' Harry pocketed the money gratefully. 'You've saved my bacon. Let's hope it comes off.'

Just then, Freddie popped his head through the door to remind him that his meal was ready, just in time to hear Prince's scathing verdict on their conversation. 'You'll never get the job with a name like that.'

Harry coughed, trying to cover up the unexpected interruption, hoping it would pass unnoticed.

'Your secret is safe with me,' he assured his friend loudly, hoping the comment would go unnoticed.

As the two of them departed, the sergeant looked after Freddie and scratched his head, perplexed. 'Now, how the devil did his friend hear about that?'

# 4

## GOING UNDERCOVER

Harry was uncertain about how he would be greeted when he arrived back at his digs, but he never imagined it would be quite as bad as it turned out.

Sheila completely ignored him and Mrs M, although ignorant of the cause of the break-up, backed her up faithfully until Harry handed over his week's rent, with the promise of more to come.

'Whatever did you do to upset the poor girl?' she demanded, melting at the sight of the money.

Swearing her to secrecy, he revealed that he had been offered the opportunity to act as an undercover agent by Sergeant Matthews to infiltrate a PR company to help him solve the mystery about her debts, amongst other things, careful not to specify what those "other things" might be.

'Only, if anyone asks for me, you must remember that in future my name is Tom Smith,' he cautioned. 'He's supposed to be a cousin of mine,' he added, making it up for her benefit, seeing her bewildered expression. 'And whatever you do, don't tell anyone else, particularly Sheila.'

'Tell her about what?' she demanded, feeling more confused than ever.

'Never mind,' he said pressing her hand, 'just trust me. She's not likely to believe anything I say, anyway. And if that accountant gets in touch, tell him you're still thinking about his offer.'

'As if I would,' she replied indignantly. 'I'll tell him what he can do with his offer, after all the work I've put into the business, cheeky devil.'

'No, don't provoke him, if you can help it. We don't want him to panic and set the lawyers on you. I've got to prove he's up to no good, so we don't want him to fly off the handle or do a bunk. I don't live here under my own name anymore, if anyone asks – I'm Tom Smith, remember? Now, why don't you make yourself a nice cup of tea,' he suggested kindly, guiding her towards the kitchen, 'while I go and have a word with Prince. Just to see if he needs to go wee-wees,' he added hastily, seeing a question hovering on her lips.

Escaping, he made for his bedroom, keeping a look out for Sheila on the way in case she appeared and froze him on the spot with one of her recent icy stares. Luckily, the coast was clear and he found Prince sitting on the bed, looking browned-off.

'Don't tell me she believed that load of rubbish.' Prince curled his lips at the news. 'And what am I supposed to do while you push off for your interview? It's no good,' he decided after thinking it over, 'you'll have to take me with you.'

'Talk sense, how can I do that when I'm supposed to be Tom Smith, my cousin.'

'I know, tell them you're looking after me while he's searching for some new digs. Listen, you've got to let me come,' he appealed. 'Supposing they don't believe you and decide to bump you off, like some of the others who went missing. I've got to know who you see, so I can identify them, otherwise how could I raise the alarm if I don't know who they are?'

'You seem convinced that I'm going to cop it,' said Harry coldly. 'Why didn't you bring your magician friend along. He could have saved the day and turned them into mice or something.'

'If only I could,' said Prince sadly. 'I haven't heard a word from him since you found me. I think he's given me up. Meanwhile,' he licked his lips, 'I'm starving. Why don't we go and have a word with Mrs M and see what she's got in the larder?'

'As long as I don't have another peep out of you while we're down there,' Harry threatened.

'Not a word.'

Later, after a satisfying spread, Harry stretched out contentedly. 'That was great, Mrs M. Compliments to the chef.'

There was a distinct burp under the table as he spoke, and a voice was heard to say, 'I second that.'

Putting his plate in the sink, Mrs M was puzzled.

'Why did you have to second that, Mr Harry – I heard you the first time.'

'Out,' said Harry sternly, pointing to the door. 'Time for your wee-wees.' Before leaving, he asked hopefully, 'Is Sheila feeling any better now?'

'I took her up something earlier,' Mrs M confessed, 'and she kept on at me, wanting to know what's happening. She was so persistent, I'm afraid I did let on you were involved in some sort of private investigation, but I didn't tell her anything else, I promise.'

'Good, I don't want her worried, that's all. Well, I'll be off, Mrs M. Don't forget to let me know tomorrow if you get any calls for Tom Smith.'

Tossing and turning in his bed that night, Harry found it difficult to get to sleep. Every time he began to drop off, the furious face of Sheila appeared accusingly in his dreams, telling him where to keep his Saucy Sue, in no uncertain terms. Finally, exhausted, he closed his eyes, only to be woken what seemed like only five minutes later by the shrill tones of the alarm clock going off.

Staggering into the bathroom, he peered at the bleary image that confronted him and sluiced his face, forcing himself to get back into the land of the living.

After snatching a quick breakfast, he was just about to reach out for the coffee pot when he heard the phone ring in the hallway and Mrs M answering. 'No, dear,' she was saying, 'nobody of that name here.'

'Who is it?' he gulped, dashing to the phone and almost snatching it out of her hands. 'Tom Smith, did you say? That's me. Could I come to an interview in an hour? Where's that – in the High Street, opposite the Town Hall? Who shall I ask for? Right.' He scribbled down a name. 'I'll be there, thank you.' He put back the receiver, sighing with relief. 'I think I'll have that coffee now, Mrs M.'


After refreshing himself and wearing a smart suit he kept for special occasions, Harry ordered a taxi, feeling that at last he could afford it, and arrived with Prince at his destination at the appointed hour. Slightly over awed by the discreet and luxurious surroundings, he gave his name at the reception desk and after checking his name, he was ushered into an office at the end of a corridor.

'Would you like me to look after your dog?' enquired the reception clerk distantly, as Prince eyed his surroundings suspiciously.

'No thanks, he gets very excitable if we're parted,' said Harry hastily.

'Ah, Mr Smith, good of you to come at such short notice.' A short, chunky looking man got up to greet him. 'Let me introduce myself. I'm Alastair Brown, head of recruitment, take a seat.' He eyed Prince somewhat doubtfully and continued, 'I gather you have applied to join our public relations department, in answer to our recent advertisement.' He consulted a letter in front of him. 'I see from your application that you have had some experience in that direction – could you give me some more details?'

'Of course.' Harry glibly recited from memory the crib that Sergeant Matthews had prepared.

'That all seems satisfactory,' acknowledged the other. 'I see you have specialised in the technique of presenting the client to his best advantage. That is a most desirable quality, as far as we are concerned.'

Harry nodded with suitable modesty. 'I do my best, but it's not been easy at times, as I expect you know.'

'I see we understand each other,' his interviewer said with feeling. 'We have that all the time with some of our clients.' He checked the letter again. 'I see that you are staying at the local board and lodging establishment, run by a Mrs Merton. Does the name Harry Bell mean anything to you – I understand he is a friend of the landlady, staying there.'

Harry tugged at Prince's lead to quieten him and crossed his fingers. 'That's right, he's a cousin of mine. He let me have his rooms while he's looking for another place. Directly he heard she was in a spot of bother he decided to move elsewhere. Very restless chap, he is.'

'It's interesting you should say that,' the other remarked dryly. 'When one of my clients saw you arrive just now, he said you bore a remarkable resemblance to this man, Bell, I believe he's called.'

'That's not unusual,' said Harry, swallowing. 'I've got dozens of people who look like me, it runs in the family.'

'Does that mean you are a close friend of the landlady as well?' pressed the other.

'Mrs Merton? I hardly know her,' lied Harry. 'She's a funny old bird, comes up with some weird ideas from time to time. Got this bee in her bonnet that her accountant chap is doing his best to ruin her. Sounds as if she needs to be locked up. Mad as a hatter, if you ask me.'

'I'm glad you see it that way,' said Mr Brown, relaxing at the news. 'I think you might be just the man we're looking for. Before you go, I'd like you to meet one of our clients you could be representing.' He pressed a bell on his desk. 'Ah, Mary, would you ask your manager to join me for a moment. Oh, he's been called away, has he? Then perhaps he could ring me when he returns. Thank you.' He replaced the receiver and turned apologetically. 'I'm afraid he's not available just now, after all. Thank you for coming along so promptly. We'll be getting in touch in the next few days. It all looks very promising. Meanwhile, take my card, keep in touch. I'm anxious to get this wrapped up as soon as possible, as I'm sure you will appreciate.'

They shook hands, Harry relieved at the thought he didn't have to meet Trustworthy, and as soon as they left the building, Prince panted. 'Thank goodness, where's the nearest lamp post – I need to do my wee-wees.'

Having sorted that problem out, Harry decided to call into the local supermarket and pick up things for lunch to celebrate. Loaded down with goodies and some flowers for Mrs M, they caught a bus that dropped them only a few yards from his lodgings.

When his landlady opened the door and saw his purchases, she cried with delight, 'Oh, my goodness, what a surprise. I was just wondering what to do about lunch. All we have is beans on toast. And flowers – who would they be for?' she asked coyly.

'Just a small thank you, Mrs M, if you could find a vase.'

'Of course, come in and tell us what's been happening.'

After a while, the delicious odours of cooking wafted up the stairs and even Sheila was persuaded to come down and join them.

It was the opportunity Harry had been waiting for. He launched into an explanation of how the girl Susan had been so grateful to him for exposing the mayor's promise to marry her as a fraud, by revealing the true extent of his infidelities. As a result, she had been searching for him everywhere, to thank him personally.

'Does this mean Mummy doesn't have to worry about that wretched accountant and those debts of hers anymore?' she asked Harry directly, still not wholly convinced by his version of events.

'Not quite that yet,' he stalled. 'But after my interview this morning, I'm almost sure I've got the job. Once I'm in, I can start finding out the truth about those accounts. The only snag is that someone might have seen me there at the interview and thought he'd recognised me. And that someone could only have been your accountant, Mrs M.'

'Oh, my word, what can we do?' She dropped her cup in her agitation, half spilling the contents.

'Don't panic,' said Harry, mopping it up. 'I pretended to be my cousin and I think I got away with it. Luckily the accountant was called away before I was introduced, so I've got myself a bit of a breather to think up something to make it sound more convincing.'

'But he was the one who saw us at that dance,' objected Sheila, giving Harry a suspicious glance at the thought of it.

'Well, it was Sergeant Matthews' idea,' he replied glibly. 'I'd better ring him and see what he has to say.'

Not only was Sergeant Matthews delighted at the way the interview had gone, but he also had some reassuring news of his own.

'You don't have to worry about that accountant for a bit. I've just heard he's been laid up, after getting involved in an accident.'

'What happened?' asked Harry, relieved at the unexpected reprieve.

'My spies were following him to see where he was going, and he was hit by a car, as he was trying to flag down a taxi. He'll be out of action for a few days I was told by the hospital, nothing too serious.'

'So, what do I do now?'

'I hear they're keen to get hold of someone, so it's my bet they'll park you onto one of the other managers until they decide where to fit you in. Keep me posted, you'll be hearing something soon,' he was promised.


The sergeant's advice was well founded. Scarcely had Harry finished breakfast the next morning when Mrs M appeared, all of a twitter. 'It's for you, Mr Harry – it's that Alastair Brown, as he calls himself.'

Waiting a minute for his nerves to calm down, he picked up the receiver. 'Tom Smith here.'

'Ah, Mr Smith, you'll be pleased to hear that your application has been successful. However, there appears to be some slight delay as to where your talents could be most usefully applied. Perhaps you could call in this afternoon sometime, say about 3 o'clock, when we might discuss the matter, if that is convenient.'

Trying not to sound too eager, Harry agreed. 'That would suit me fine. Look forward to it.'

Replacing the receiver with mixed feelings, Harry went to impart the latest news.

Mrs M was all of a flutter, concerned that he might be walking into the lion's den, as she put it, after hearing why the sergeant had selected him.

'Are you sure it's quite safe, Mr Harry,' she enquired anxiously.

'Don't worry about me, Mrs M,' he assured her, wishing he hadn't gone into quite so much detail.

'Why don't I apply for a job there as well,' urged Sheila, showing signs of softening towards him.

'I think that's the sergeant calling me,' said Harry hastily, not wanting to get her involved. 'I'll just go and see.'

By an odd coincidence, his wishful feeling turned out to be correct. Gratified to hear that it was all going as planned, the sergeant added some comforting news of his own. 'You'll be pleased to know that you won't be working alone. We've managed to get one of our women police officers taken on as a temporary secretary.'

'How will I know who she is?' asked Harry quickly, relieved to know he would have a contact in case of an emergency.

'You don't need to at this stage,' replied the Sergeant cautiously. 'She'll find some way of getting in touch with you. The password is 'gammon', by the way. You'll like her,' he added with a chuckle, 'she's a real corker.'

'Thanks, Sarg.' He swallowed weakly, putting the receiver down hurriedly, in case they were overheard.

*That's all I need to know,* he thought. If that was all he had to worry about, he might have got away with a solo reconnaissance to see what he was up against, but he had reckoned without Prince.

'And where do you think you're going?' The familiar voice halted him in his tracks as he made for the front door.

'Oh no, not you as well,' he groaned. Checking his watch, he made a quick decision. 'Come into the bedroom and I'll explain...'

'...so, you see, there's no need for you to come along. The sergeant has fixed me up with a contact once I'm inside, in case of emergencies,' he finished.

'All right, I suppose.' But as soon as Harry had gone, Prince racked his brains trying to think of some way to get in touch with his valet, Jazz, and get his advice.

Back in the kitchen, Mrs M was also undecided about what to do, but Sheila had already made up her mind. Although she still had some misgivings, she felt she couldn't let Harry go it alone without anyone to help him. She decided that she would forgive him for what had happened and be there by his side, to give him moral support.

In spite of the slight delay getting hold of a taxi, Harry managed his appointment on time and was soon ushered into reception.

Meanwhile, Mr. Brown was just finishing a call to his deputy. '...then I'll leave him in your care, Simon. He seems to have all the qualities we're looking for, but I'm not entirely convinced about his background story, so I'm relying on you to keep an eye on him. Give him something fairly simple and straightforward to get on with until Reggie gets back after that accident and is able to confirm his details. Right, must go, he's just arrived.'

Overhearing the last part of the conversation expressing reservations about his background, Harry felt a trifle nervous as he was ushered in.

Rising to his feet, Alastair Brown welcomed him. 'Ah, here you are, Mr Smith. I've just been speaking to my deputy, Simon, who will be joining us shortly. He will be looking after you for a week or so to get you settled in, while we find out a suitable position for you... and here he is.'

Harry got up with a prepared smile, but the sight of the newcomer quickly wiped it off his face. It was the same man he'd passed after leaving Superintendent Morrison's office earlier, wearing the uniform of a police officer. Masking the shock, he held out a hand. 'How do you do.'

A flicker of puzzled politeness appeared for a moment on the other's face. 'Hello, Mr Smith – I'm elected to show you around. My name is Simon Shaw. If you'd like to come to my office, I'll put you in the picture.'

Harry followed him in a daze, trying to work out what was going on, as the other briskly led the way.

His second shock was when they passed an attractive young lady in the corridor, who stood to one side and flashed a smile at him, before whispering the magic password "gammon", as she did so.

'That was Rachel, who will be working for you as your new secretary, by the way,' his host remarked casually over his shoulder, as they entered his office. 'Rachel is new here as well, so it will be a good opportunity for you to get to know each other.'

When they were seated and Harry was offered a coffee, it was gradually borne on him that Mrs M's accountant, Reginald Trustworthy, as he called himself, was a key player in the firm's activities. After some delicate probing, it seemed that he was responsible for auditing the accounts of most of the company's clients. In return, Harry guessed, he probably had the full PR support and protection of the company if his integrity was questioned.

'This is where your background and experience could be most useful,' stressed his new manager. 'Reggie appears to have had some difficulty in persuading your landlady,' he checked his correspondence, 'a Mrs Merton – presumably a widow, since she appears to be living alone and has a daughter called Sheila – that she is heavily overdrawn and is unwilling to hand over the business in payment for her debts.'

He waved a hand dismissively. 'This is not uncommon in

our line of business, but usually the account turns out to be more profitable, otherwise we wouldn't normally be interested. I may be wrong, but there could be another reason in this case, possibly involving the daughter.' He chewed his pen reflectively.

'Is that why you asked me here?' asked Harry nervously, anticipating the next request.

'Exactly. What we need is someone on the spot who can find out exactly what the problem is and how we can overcome it. You would be ideally placed to act on our behalf – and it would be a useful exercise for you to start with. As soon as Mr Trustworthy is recovered and well enough to return, we can compare notes and decide on the next course of action. Meanwhile, I'll ring Rachel and get her to show you your office. Any questions?'

'No,' said Harry quickly. He couldn't wait to meet his new contact and discover more about the set up.

Waiting impatiently for Shaw to go through the introductions, he sighed with relief as soon as the door at last closed behind him and he was free to speak.

'Rachel,' he began hurriedly to his new secretary, 'I know who you are, so let's skip the formalities. Sergeant Matthews has told me all about you. I understand that Mrs Merton's accountant also handles the accounts for the mayor. How can I get hold of a copy of his accounts – do you know where he keeps them?'

She put a finger to her lips in case they were overheard. 'I haven't been here very long. I thought they might be in one of the desk drawers, but I'm told they are locked up in the office safe. Don't worry, I have a key that will open it, I keep it here.'

Just then, the door opened and Sheila peered in, right as the typist pulled up her skirt and extracted the key from her stocking top, revealing a tantalising glimpse of her tights.

'Oh good, at last I've found you,' gasped Sheila thankfully

as she entered, then catching sight of Rachel she clutched at the door. 'HARRY, not again. How could you!'

Wheeling around, Harry found his voice and stuttered. 'I only wanted to know where he keeps them...'

'So, I see,' she said bitingly. 'The first place anyone would look.'

'You don't understand,' he cried desperately. 'It wasn't in her drawers – she was just showing me...'

'You don't have to explain,' she cried witheringly. 'And I thought I could trust you. That's it, as far as I'm concerned. Get lost!' With a choked cry, she rushed out, slamming the door behind her.

# 5

## RIPE FOR PLUNDERING

'Oh dear,' said Rachel, after a pregnant pause. 'Is that your girlfriend?'

'She was,' Harry corrected moodily.

'What do we do now?' She held out the key. 'Do you still want this?'

Forcing himself to think after the bombshell that had just hit him, he gathered what was left of his wits. 'Yes, of course. If you could run off a copy of the accounts, I'll see if I can get them checked out.'

While he waited, he reviewed the impossible position he now found himself in. As well as losing the love of his life yet again, Mrs M was relying on him to find some way of proving her accounts had been faked, and at the same time he was expected by his new boss to push the deal through, an unwelcome course of action that would probably land his landlady back in the soup.

'Quick, let me have the copy,' he panted. 'I will get the Superintendent to have a look, tell the sergeant.'

. . .

'So, there was a connection after all,' said Super when consulted, after comparing the two versions. 'Who would have believed it, a respectable figure like that. Now that we've got all this extra information, it begins to tally up. As you see, his debts started piling up after he took over the hotel, when all those girlfriends started costing him the earth; then along comes your Mrs M with a thriving little business and bingo, his problems are solved.'

'But that wouldn't account for the massive difference in costs,' objected Harry. 'The hotel expenses must be enormous, compared with Mrs M's.'

'Ah, well once he got the idea, your accountant must have discovered some other handy accounts ripe for plundering, landing them in the same sticky situation. This is not the first time I've come across the practice, you'd be surprised. My office would be covered from floor to ceiling with all the frauds I've encountered.'

'How do we prove it?'

'That's going to be your next problem,' the Super said. 'What you need is an excuse to worm yourself into his business somehow and get your hands on the evidence. You'll need to do it soon,' he pointed out, 'before Trustworthy gets back, otherwise you'll find it more difficult.'

'That's what I was hoping to do,' said Harry, 'but the nearest I got, after the sergeant wangled it, was the mayor's office.'

'That's a good start,' encouraged the Super. 'It will give you the opportunity of looking through the files and get to know the business. Once you've done that, it will give you a good excuse to search elsewhere.'

'The other problem is that the accountant has got himself injured in a car accident and won't be back for a week or so,' Harry said, 'which means I can't get into his office to check on anything. That reminds me.' He thought back. 'After I called on you the other day, I ran into someone called Simon Shaw. Does the name mean anything to you?'

He waited hopefully for a reaction and saw a note of cautious recognition register on his friend's face.

'Ah yes, but he doesn't want too many to know about him. He's one of our special branch people, and uses a number of different aliases when he's acting undercover. I should watch your step where he's concerned – you never know what you might get into. Take my advice and steer clear.'

Harry was bewildered. 'Are you sure about this? I can't afford to make a mistake at this stage of the game.'

'Absolutely. If you have any doubts, ask that Sergeant of yours – he would know.'

'I will. Wonder why he didn't tell me about him before?'

'I was keeping him up my sleeve,' admitted Sergeant Matthews when Harry put the question to him later. 'I wasn't sure how the plan was going to work.'

'But don't you see what an awkward position you've put me in?' Harry appealed. 'I don't know if it's safe to let him know who I am. You've left me right in it. I don't know whether I'm standing on my head or my heels.'

'You look all right to me, where I'm sitting,' the sergeant summed up with a chuckle after a critical glance. 'Seems to me, you're in an ideal position. All you have to do now is to get him to transfer you to Trustworthy's office and you can start finding out what's behind it all.'

'What excuse have I got? That Shaw manager wants me to go to my digs to check it out and prove it's all above board. Am I supposed to reveal I know who he really is?'

'No, that wouldn't help us at this stage. Don't forget he's been told to keep an eye on you, because his boss doesn't entirely trust you. The only way you're going to prove those accounts are faked is to carry out an on-the-spot investigation in his office, before Trustworthy gets back and recognises you.'

'That's all very well,' said Harry glancing at his watch and wincing at the memory of Sheila's outburst. 'It's too late now to do much probing. I must get back and see if I can make some sort of peace with Sheila, if she'll listen.' He shuddered at the thought of what she might say.

'Good luck,' said his friend in sympathy. 'Take her some flowers, that sometimes does the trick.'

'I'm afraid it'll take more than that to make her see sense.'

Bearing in mind his friend's suggestion, Harry made his way back to his digs, loaded down with more goodies than anyone would expect in the circumstances.

As well as an armful of flowers, he staggered in with a hamper packed with enough food for an army. Unfortunately, it was not enough to persuade his heart's desire to put even one foot outside her bedroom door. As Mrs M put it bluntly, 'You've really gone and done it this time, Mr Harry.'

However much he suffered from the rebuff, he did his best to ignore it, hoping that eventually she would relent and forgive him. What he could not ignore was the evident relish that Prince made of the unexpected windfall. He was so puffed out with all the treats on offer, it almost made him forget to complain that he had been deserted the best part of the day, and had missed all the action.

It wasn't until Harry had let him out and locked up for the day, that his grievances returned when they retired for the night.

'So what have I missed?' he asked, after polishing off a meat roll he'd overlooked. 'Don't keep it to yourself.' When Harry at last was forced to admit about his confrontation with Sheila, he hooted, 'There you are, if I'd have been with you, I could have kept watch outside and warned you in time.'

However wounding his remark, it struck home and gave Harry an idea. If he was going to do the job properly tomorrow, without fear of being interrupted, that's exactly what he would need to do.

'You're on,' he agreed before settling down and switching off the light. All he needed to do now was to persuade his boss to switch him over to work in Trustworthy's office.

In the event, it turned out to be easier than he had expected. Looking up briefly from his papers, Simon Shaw just nodded at his request. 'Go ahead, it will give you a better idea of the work load once you start there. Mary, his secretary, is away at the moment, so why don't you take young Rachel with you if you like, all good experience.'

'No, if you don't mind, I'll leave her until I've sorted things out,' Harry said hastily, turning pale at the thought of Sheila finding out.

'Please yourself. Oh, and take that poodle of yours with you. Can't stand him staring at me all the time.'

Harry yanked at the lead, hoping Prince would get the message, but was too late to prevent him uttering a farewell response, 'You're no oil painting yourself, buster.'

'What was that you said?' Shaw jerked his head around, not sure if he had heard correctly. 'Oh, he's gone, must be my imagination, I could have sworn...'

Despite the fact that he had turned down Shaw's offer, all his feverish excuses proved a waste of time and Rachel turned up as usual, much to his annoyance. 'But I'll have to come with you,' she insisted. 'I'm the only one who knows how to open the safe.'

So Harry carried on hopefully with Prince in tow to safeguard his retreat. This time, Rachel was waiting to open the door and thankfully not a sign of Sheila could be seen. He began to relax and was beginning to dismiss any fears as imagination when he received an alert from his faithful guard dog at his heels. As he entered, he received an urgent aside from Prince who whispered, 'I should watch that secretary of yours, I think she's got her eye on you.'

'Nonsense,' he replied lightly. 'She says she's got something to show me.'

'That's what I mean,' warned the other significantly.

'Absolute rot.' Harry brushed away any doubts he might have. 'She's promised to open everything up for me.'

'Exactly.'

Once inside Trustworthy's office, he breathed more freely and got down to checking all the desk drawers for Mrs M's accounts as the first step. He knew that if he didn't find some explanation for the huge difference in the figures he was wasting his time. Drawing a blank, he turned to ask Rachel to open the safe and found she was already sorting out the contents.

'See if there's anything for a Mrs Merton, that's my landlady,' he began. 'We'll need that to start with...'

Rachel combed through the papers as he spoke. 'Yes, you're lucky. There seem to be lots of other accounts as well, including an earlier one for the hotel that's completely overdrawn. Wow, look at those figures, they're enormous.'

'Is there a more recent one of the hotel accounts, showing it back in credit?' he persisted. 'Hang on, perhaps I'd better have a look.'

'Wait a minute, I've found another one.' She got excited. 'Yes, you're right. Some credits been added in quite recently.'

'Is there another one showing any transfers between the two accounts? Here, pass them over and let me see.'

'Now, this is interesting,' she said, ignoring his request as she delved deeper. 'Yes, there seems to be some sort of connection...'

'Well, don't keep it to yourself,' urged Harry, losing his patience. 'Let me have a look.'

But Rachel didn't appear to be listening and instead deliberately misinterpreted his remark. Looking up, she said coyly, 'What do I get in exchange?'

'What do you mean? Sergeant Matthews promised you would help me.'

'I was beginning to wonder when you'd notice me, for a change,' she said, getting down from the safe and advancing on him invitingly. 'Now that I know Sheila has lost interest, I thought I might fill the gap, if you know what I mean.' She gave him a seductive glance, hoping to encourage him.

'Of course, your advice is naturally welcome,' he said hastily, wilfully misunderstanding her invitation.

'So, what do I get out of it?' she asked lazily, slowly undoing the top button of her blouse.

'Why, I shall mention you in my report, naturally,' added Harry, nervously.

'Watch it!' warned Prince.

'Is that all?' she asked, undoing another button.

'I'll say you gave me every help,' he added hastily.

She finished unbuttoning her blouse and slipped the top half off. 'Like this?'

'Why, what were you expecting?' He looked away, pretending not to notice.

Rachel moved a little closer. 'I was hoping you might find me attractive.'

'I do, I do.' He gulped, edging backwards.

Casting her blouse aside, she tiptoed up to him and slid a hand over his chest. 'Did I tell you, I find you awfully handsome?' Her hand dropped to his waist and drew him towards her in a close embrace.

'Wait a minute.' He pulled away desperately. 'You've got it all wrong. I just feel like a... father towards you.'

She reached up and kissed his cheek. 'Kiss me properly then, Daddy, and I might let you see that report, and anything else you might fancy.'

He gave her a peck that he hoped would satisfy her and held out his hand hopefully for the accounts.

'Call that a kiss?' she said disparagingly. 'Give me something I can remember you by.'

Coming to his aid, Prince smartly nipped her ankle to divert her attention.

'Oh,' she cried, 'that's not what I meant at all.' Rubbing her ankle, she ignored the assault and clasped him firmly in her arms. 'If you want to play rough, big boy, I'll show you how I really feel.'

As they struggled backwards and forwards, the door opened unexpectedly behind them and a voice demanded fiercely, 'What the devil's going on in here?'

Startled, they fell apart and Harry looked around dazedly. Before he could utter a word of protest, Prince decided to distract the man's attention and bit him on his ankle as well.

'Ouch. He attacked me,' fumed the newcomer. 'What do think you're doing, bringing that confounded dog in here. Who are you?'

'And what's it to you, nosy?' retaliated Prince loudly, trying to get to his other ankle.

'Good God, a damned ventriloquist, as well. What do you mean by invading my office without permission?'

'Your office?' repeated Harry, pulling himself together at the shock of seeing who it was. He panicked, pretending not to recognise the face. 'Do I know you?'

'I happen to be Mr Trustworthy, and this is my office – and

who, may I ask, are you? And more to the point, what is that young lady doing here, half undressed?'

'Ah, well it's like this,' gabbled Harry, trying to think of a convincing excuse. 'I was asked by Mr Shaw to come and work here, while I get to know the routine. My name is Tom Smith and I've just joined the staff, Rachel here will tell you...'

'Wait a minute,' interrupted Trustworthy, as it all became clear in his mind, 'I remember where I've seen you before. It was when I was checking the accounts with Mrs Merton and I saw you dancing with her daughter. I know who you are. You're not Tom Smith... you're...'

Harry's trained mind registered the sound of a gunshot before the man's voice was cut off abruptly and he slumped forward in a crumpled heap.

## 6

# HIS OWN IDEAS

After the initial shock wore off, Harry's police training came to his aid and took over. 'Quick,' he instructed Rachel, 'give me a hand to lay him out on that sofa.'

He felt Trustworthy's pulse and reaching for the phone, rang for help. 'Hello? Yes, it's an emergency, I need an ambulance at the double. A man has been shot... yes, in our office. He's still alive, as far as I can see. Where?' He rattled off the address, added a few more details then rang off. 'Now for the police, Sergeant Matthews, I think.'

While he waited, a thought occurred. He waved a hand at Rachel who sat shaken at the sudden turn of events, her blouse back on and all thoughts of any romantic engagement wiped from her mind. 'We'd better get those accounts together ready to show him, before someone decides to hide them away.'

They didn't have to wait very long. With a screech of brakes, an ambulance pulled up outside and a flurry of footsteps on the stairs announced the arrival of a doctor and his assistant. Shortly afterwards, a car drew up and Sergeant Matthews bustled in, accompanied by a senior officer. After a quick examination with his stethoscope, the doctor gave his verdict. 'His

heart is very weak. Let's get him to the hospital right away.'
With a nod to his assistant, the doctor helped to place the
wounded patient onto a stretcher and made for the exit.

'Wait a minute, where are you taking him?' asked Harry
anxiously. 'We'll want to know where to get in touch.'

'If I can request your attention,' broke in the commanding
voice of the new arrival. 'Perhaps you would be good enough to
make the introductions, Sergeant.'

As the wail of the ambulance died away, Sergeant Matthews
hurriedly ushered forward his companion whose brusque and
demanding appearance made Harry forget for a moment about
the doctor's hasty departure.

'Let me introduce Inspector Pain, who has been appointed
to take charge of the case, in view of the circumstances. I have
given him a full explanation of the situation, but no doubt he
will form his own ideas,' the sergeant added apologetically with
a slight shake of his head, giving a hint of his own personal feelings on the choice.

'*Chief* Inspector Pain,' the other corrected stiffly, making it
quite clear who was in charge. 'Having weighed up the
evidence, it is obvious to me who the culprit is, the landlady
who calls herself Mrs Merton, or someone acting on her
behalf.'

'What? You must be joking,' burst out Harry, totally bewildered, about to hand over the accounts. 'How do you make that
out?'

'She is the only one who would benefit from the attack,' the
inspector insisted, drawing himself up stiffly. 'It is quite obvious,' he repeated, 'even to a blind man.'

'But you haven't even met her, how can you be so sure?' He
looked at Sergeant Matthews for support and received a help-
less nod in agreement.

'Please do not question my judgement.' Before Harry could
put up any more arguments, he went on, 'Our next step is to

question this Mrs Merton to see what she has to say for herself. Where can she be found?'

'In Tanfield, a few miles down the road, she's my landlady,' explained Harry. As the enormity of the accusation struck him, he defended her warmly.

'But she'd never dream of doing anything like that. What grounds do you have for such a...' "Mad" was the word he was about to use, but seeing the set expression on the inspector's face, he substituted, saying instead, 'such an extraordinary idea?'

'On the contrary, there is nothing "extraordinary" about it, as you put it,' he was informed coldly. 'I asked myself, who is the person who would most likely benefit from such an attack? Answer, Mrs Merton. She is heavily in debt, as a result of his handling of her accounts. I should have thought that it was quite obvious. Since you are a tenant, kindly inform the landlady in question that I wish to see her here at the scene of the crime at precisely two o'clock this afternoon. Meanwhile, I'll get my assistant, Sergeant Winkle, to run a check on her. That is all.' With that, he swept out, leaving an awed silence behind him.

'Where on earth did he come from?' was all Harry could manage.

'He's one of the chief's latest recruits,' offered the sergeant heavily. 'He hasn't been with us very long, more's the pity. The last fella he nabbed was a raving loony and couldn't wait to give himself up, and the inspector's been trading on that ever since, a right pain he is an' all.'

'I'd better go and break the news to Mrs M,' decided Harry. 'She'll need all the support she can get.'

'You do that, and the best of luck,' sympathised the sergeant. 'I'll let you know how Trustworthy is the moment I hear. Meanwhile, give my regards to Mrs M.'

       ·  ·  ·

When Harry got to his digs, he found the place was agog with rumours.

'It was on the news,' confirmed Mrs M, all of a twitter. 'That poor man. Heaven knows, I couldn't bear the sight of him – but getting shot and ending up in hospital, I ask you. Do we know how he is?'

'Not in very good shape apparently,' admitted Harry distractedly, nerving himself up to breaking the news about the interview facing her. 'The inspector has asked if you could have a word with him this afternoon – he's got some bee in his bonnet about everyone's movements at the time of the shooting. Nothing to worry about,' he said hurriedly. 'I'll be there to back you up, just a formality.'

'I should hope so,' said Mrs M indignantly. 'Worst thing I ever did, letting that man see my accounts.'

When Sheila heard about the summons, she was up in arms immediately. 'How dare he think that of Mummy, of all the nerve, silly man. I know, I'll say I was there, just to be awkward – that would put a stop to it.'


As soon as his sergeant was informed of her intentions, he passed it on to his superior.

'Her daughter's involved as well, is she?' he barked. 'What do we know about her, Sergeant Winkle?'

'Nothing in the records, sir. She lives at home and gives a hand with the tenants, I understand.'

'Hm, well call her in first and we'll see if their stories match up.'


'A man, you say, what did he look like?' he demanded suspiciously when she was brought before him.

Racking her brain for a plausible answer, Sheila thought

furiously. 'It was definitely a man,' she said slowly, spinning out the suspense, hoping it would divert his attention away from her mother. Seeing his look of disbelief she fibbed, 'with a hat worn over his eyes. That was all I could see,' she ended hopefully.

'Nothing else? Height?' he insisted, frustrated.

'About your height,' she added, beginning to resent his attitude. 'Nothing to write home about.'

'Thank you,' he said frigidly, 'that is all for the moment.'

After she had left, satisfied she had done her bit to put the inspector off, she muttered to herself, 'What an officious little man.'

The inspector was not satisfied. He rounded on his sergeant afterwards. 'She's covering up. Let's see what her mother has to say. I mean to get to the bottom of this.'

Fortunately, when it came to it, Mrs M was able to provide a cast iron alibi of her movements for the time in question which left him even more frustrated. News of her financial plight had already spread through the village and a number of local tradesmen had turned up to demand payment for services rendered, including a hefty butcher's bill and one of equal proportions from the baker and fishmonger, all of which covered the time span involved, much to the inspector's annoyance.

When Sheila arrived back from her interrogation she was piqued to learn that her intervention wasn't necessary after all. 'If I'd have known,' she railed, 'I would have told him where to get off.'

'Never mind, love,' her mother sympathised. 'You weren't to know and don't forget, you have to be polite to the police. Anyway, I was in the clear, so that's all right, we can forget about it.'

'You don't understand,' Sheila insisted. 'I could see he didn't believe a word I said. He won't give up, he's got it in for us.'

'I tell you what,' said her mother, inspired. 'Why don't we have a word with Harry? He'll think of something.'

'Don't mention that name to me,' flared her daughter. 'I've finished with him.'

'There, there, why don't you sit down while I make us a nice cup of tea,' soothed Mrs M, making her mind up privately to seek advice elsewhere.


But although fully in agreement with her sentiments, Harry was equally baffled. Everyone was expecting him to do something, but – what? he asked himself. He was in an impossible position, stuck between two camps and no one he could immediately turn to. What was he to do? The only person he knew who wasn't involved in this ghastly situation was... his uncle. Of course, why didn't he think of that before? He might even know something about this new inspector who had been foisted on them.

Settled in his mind as to his next step, he wasted no more time and immediately contacted his relative.

'As I see it,' said Uncle Ted when consulted, 'now that this accountant is out of the way, your next bet is to have a word with his secretary as soon as she gets back. She's bound to have details of all his contacts and she'll probably be able to spill the beans on what he gets up to on the quiet. This is the opportunity you've been waiting for.'

He paused to reflect. 'As for that new inspector...' He shook his head. 'I reckon the chief's gone off his rocker over him. Before I retired, he was like a raw recruit you might say, still green as they come. He's got the right name, "Pain", it described him exactly. How he managed to get where he is today, I shall never know. He was a proper little know-all, as he was fond of telling us.'

'He still is,' said Harry with feeling, 'from what I've seen of him so far. He even accused my landlady. It was a good thing she had an alibi when Trustworthy was attacked. Not content with that,' he said, 'he tried to implicate that nice daughter of hers. Luckily it didn't work.'

'I wouldn't be too sure about that. He's a vain little squirt and pompous with it. He doesn't like being thwarted if he thinks his judgement is being questioned.'

As he spoke, the phone rang and he picked the receiver up. 'Hello? Yes, speaking. Is that you, Jimmy?' His face lit up. 'You old devil, why haven't I heard from you before now? It seems ages. Yes, he's with me at this moment.' His smile slipped. 'Yes, I'll tell him. Gone missing, did you say? When was this, soon after he was admitted? Where was the hospital and what excuse did they give? Yes, I'll tell him. Okay, cheers for now, make it soon.'

He put the phone down soberly. 'That was Jimmy,' adding, 'Sergeant Matthews, to you. I'm afraid Trustworthy's disappeared. Apparently, the ambulance carted him off somewhere and nobody knows where. There's a general alert out for him. That inspector is hopping mad about it all. He's fuming, and just after he's taken over, as well.'

'Let's hope he knows what he's doing,' sighed Harry. 'Come on, Prince,' he decided, forgetting his uncle was present. 'Time we looked up that secretary of his and find out what she has to say.'

'That's funny.' Uncle Ted shook his head sadly after they left. 'He's started talking to himself now, poor lad. It gets you in the end. Hm, from what he was saying, he seems to be getting quite a reputation with the ladies as well. I hope he knows what he's doing, particularly where that inspector is concerned. I must keep an eye on things and find out what's going on, in case he needs some help.'

.  .  .

Back at Police HQ, Colonel Slaughter, the Chief Constable of the County, was of the same opinion and decided it was time to find out for himself what was going on. He was not satisfied with how events were shaping up. His new inspector might well be pleased with the turn of events, but he certainly was not. 'Tell the inspector to report to me at once,' he barked at the receiver.

Within minutes, his subordinate appeared and sprang to attention. 'Sir.'

'What's the latest on this Trustworthy case. I hear the man's been shot and disappeared on the way to the hospital. Have you rounded up any suspects?'

The inspector couldn't wait to vent his suspicions. 'Acting on information received, I interviewed the lady who would benefit most from his passing, the landlady, Mrs Merton,' he intoned, 'but she managed to find witnesses who supported her version of events at the time of the incident.' His curt dismissal of their evidence spoke volumes about his own views on the subject.

'And who were they?'

'A local butcher, a fishmonger and the village baker, who were owed money,' he said grudgingly.

'Anything else?'

'I was not impressed by the account given by her daughter, Miss Sheila, who claimed she saw the intruder, sir.'

'Did her description give you any lead?'

'No, sir, it definitely did not. I think she deliberately tried to put us off the scent.'

'I suppose she would do, we can't blame her for that,' decided the Chief Constable, trying for once to be fair, knowing how his own daughter would have behaved under similar circumstances. 'Is there anyone else you have in mind?'

'Yes, sir, there most definitely is. If you remember, one of the landlady's lodgers is a certain Harry Bell, a former Police

Constable who was dismissed from his post after committing a gross offence.'

'Yes, well we won't go into that,' interrupted his superior hastily. 'I gather that Sergeant Matthews has a high regard for his potential abilities though – perhaps we overlooked something there. I hear that he has been given an assignment working undercover on a recent investigation.'

The inspector was not impressed. 'That is so,' he conceded. 'But I gather that no new evidence has come to light to support such a step. To my mind,' he ventured stiffly, 'a wholly unnecessary exercise.'

'We shall have to wait and see,' decided the Chief Constable. 'If he takes after his uncle, he may well surprise us yet.'

'If you say so, sir,' accepted the inspector woodenly, unconvinced.

'Meanwhile, I assume you've put out a general alert about the missing accountant. Do we have a description, or any other details about him, in case he should turn up?'

'No, sir, he was taken away before I had a chance,' the inspector excused himself stiffly. 'If you remember, that young ex-constable, Harry Bell, let the ambulance go without confirming where they were taking the patient.'

'Don't forget, you were there at the time, if I remember rightly, and had the same opportunity,' reminded Colonel Slaughter sharply, annoyed at the inspector's attitude. 'Well, have a word with Trustworthy's doctor to see if he has anything on his records. Let's hope we will find out something soon, otherwise people will be asking awkward questions. I must contact Sergeant Matthews and see if that young friend of his has come up with anything.'

Meanwhile, fortified by his uncle's backing, Harry returned to Trustworthy's office with Prince in tow, to be confronted by a police guard and asked in no uncertain terms to prove his identity. After several phone calls were made, he was reluctantly admitted to the office and was ushered into the reception area past the desk, now festooned with tape where the accountant had been shot.

To his relief, the young receptionist was not the dreaded Rachel, as he had feared, but a quiet and unassuming young lady who announced herself as Mary, Trustworthy's secretary.

Using his newly acquired alias of Tom Smith, Harry bluffed his way through, explaining that he was working undercover to investigate the disappearance of her manager, with full permission of his superior, Simon Shaw.

Suitably impressed and visibly shaken by recent events, Mary asked how she could help.

Taking the bull by the horns, Harry launched into a summary of what was known about her late manager's activities, skating over the fraudulent aspects and concentrating instead on his known contacts.

Trying her best to help, the young secretary confessed that she had not been in the post all that long and racked her brains to conjure up a list that would satisfy him. None of the names and descriptions made any immediate sense, and after checking the time, Harry made up his mind on the spur of the moment and suggested they could continue the discussion over lunch.

Flattered by his attention, Mary accepted willingly and accompanied him to a cosy little restaurant around the corner. Bored by the endless questions, Prince happily accepted some nibbles and settled down for a quiet doze under the table.

Unsure how to broach the subject and hoping her tongue might be loosened with the help of a glass of wine, Harry waved his hand for service and nearly fell off his seat when he thought he heard a familiar voice behind him announcing her presence.

'You called?' the voice behind him enquired frostily.

Harry gulped. He could have sworn it sounded just like

Sheila's, but of course it couldn't be, she was looking after her mother. Wake up, he told himself. The possibility it conjured up had such a damaging effect on his morale however, it was enough to put him off his stroke.

Keeping his head down, he moistened his lips. 'What would you like, Mary?' he asked, rapidly revising in his mind the list of tempting items on the menu that would have made his task easier.

To his relief, his companion smiled happily. 'Just an omelette for me, thanks.'

'And what about you, sir?' the voice enquired temptingly. 'A drink to go with it?'

'Good gracious no, an omelette would be fine,' he assured the waitress hastily, not daring to look to see who it was.

As her figure melted into the background, he mopped his forehead feverishly, doing his best to blot out the unexpected intrusion that made him forget for a moment the purpose of his visit.

'You were asking me about contacts,' his companion prompted, as his attention seemed to wander.

'Yes, forgive me,' he apologised, wondering how he was going to explain his latest meeting to Sheila, or 'dalliance', as she would no doubt call it when he saw her again, which at the moment seemed unlikely, thank heavens.

'Contacts,' Mary reminded him gently, seeing his somewhat dazed expression.

The mention of contacts, for some reason, sparked off a recollection of an earlier conversation he'd had with Sergeant Matthews about "wanted" leaflets and brought him back to life.

It was worth a try. Casting doubts aside, he rummaged in his inside pocket and pulled out a crumpled leaflet.

'I don't suppose this face would mean anything to you?'

Taking a closer look, she looked puzzled. 'It's funny you should ask that. If it wasn't for that beard, I would have said there was more than a passing resemblance to my manager, Mr Trustworthy.'

Harry jumped at the mention of the name. Taking a second look, Mary corrected herself. 'What am I talking about? The name's quite different isn't it, and he looks so much younger in that picture.'

'It was probably taken some time ago, when he was on the run,' replied Harry absently, then as the idea took shape in his mind, he did a rethink. Of course, that would account for the change in the man's appearance, as the picture showed. 'With that beard gone, it makes all the difference,' he announced gleefully. His excitement was infectious.

'Does that mean he was working under an assumed name?' She peered at the picture to make sure. 'You mean, he's not my Mr Trustworthy after all, but... someone calling himself "M.T. Banks"?' She giggled as she tried to pronounce it. 'It sounds like empty banks.' She peered at the leaflet in disbelief. 'I see, as it says here, a con artist and a fraudster?'

'Yes, it could be,' he commented soberly. 'Of course, we'll know for sure if we can match physical characteristics, but if it's true,' his eyes lit up, 'it means Mrs M whose accounts he audited isn't in debt after all. She never has been!'

Mary clasped her hands. 'Oh, I'm so pleased for her sake, poor woman. What a weight off her mind. Is she a friend of yours?'

Harry explained the background to his investigation.

The thought of being interviewed made her pause nervously. 'Does that mean I'll be asked a lot of questions?'

'Nothing to worry about,' he assured her. Then as the significance of the poster dawned on him, he asked casually, 'I suppose none of these other leaflets mean anything to you?' He delved into his pocket as he spoke and produced several more. 'What about this one, and this?'

The first one produced no reaction at all and he was about

to put them back with a sigh of resignation when she clutched his arm excitedly. 'Wait a minute, I remember that other one, he had a scar on the side of his face, just like that.' She touched Harry's face impulsively to emphasize the point and ran her hand across his cheek to show him where she was thinking.

'You mean just there?' He pressed her hand at the exact spot shown in the leaflet just to confirm it, when an icy voice broke into the conversation.

'Don't move, Prince Charming. I'd like that for my photo album, if you don't mind.'

Glancing up, Harry found himself gazing into the furious face of Sheila.

Hearing his name mentioned, the dog stirred at his feet and woke up. 'Did someone call?'

In the midst of all the recriminations, Sheila pointed her camera at Mary scornfully. 'Ask your latest friend to come a little closer, so I can see who she is. I have a special place in my album for all your girlfriends.'

Harry held up his arms in protest, trying to explain. 'You don't understand. Mary here has just confirmed that Trustworthy was a swindler as I suspected and was trying to take over your mother's business. You should be *thanking* her, not accusing her of anything.'

Sheila halted in her tracks. 'Is this true?' she demanded fiercely, changing her tune.

Shaken by her attitude, Mary stood up and took a step forward uncertainly. 'I didn't know, truly I didn't. He took me in as well. His real name so it says here, is M.T. Banks, some kind of con man.'

Taken aback at the unexpected revelation, Sheila sprang forward to embrace her.

Thinking she was about to be assaulted, Mary stepped back nervously, nearly tripping over her chair. 'No, I was talking about Mr Trustworthy, my manager,' she explained hurriedly.

'I take it all back, darling,' cried Sheila excitedly, throwing her arms around Harry as well. 'I can't wait to tell Mummy. What are we waiting for?'

Meanwhile, the lady in question had been busy, sizing up the situation. Now it appeared that her accountant was no longer around to pester her with his demands, she felt a load had been lifted off her shoulders. What she had to do, she realised, was to make up her mind about the future and decide how to get her cherished business back on its feet again. She had to face the facts.

Since she was forced to let her staff go and find positions elsewhere, it left her with a problem that had to be solved. She could no longer sit back and plan the future with any degree of certainty. She was past the age when she was able to run the business single-handed, like she used to. The solution was obvious, she needed help, but where could she get it? She had managed for a while with the help of her daughter, but after that bust-up with Harry, the poor girl was mooning around the place like a lost soul.

No, the answer was staring her in the face. Now that she could rely on a steady income from Harry with his new job, she could afford to take on staff, even if it meant employing someone part-time. She fished out a copy of the local rag and scanned the advertisements. Quickly jotting down her basic requirements, she phoned the newspaper and sat back waiting for results.

It was not long in coming. Before she knew where she was, the applications came in thick and fast with surprising speed, much to her bewilderment, as if someone had seized an advanced copy almost before the advertisement had a chance to appear on the news stand in the High Street.

Wading through the applications, Mrs M dropped the

obvious rejects in the wastepaper basket and was about to give up when there was a discreet knock on the door. Summoning up her remaining strength, she tottered to open it. On the mat stood a middle-aged, respectable looking gentleman, holding a tureen in his hands.

He offered her a spoon. 'Would Madam care to try my special soup?' he enquired, lifting the lid.

Dumbly, Mrs M did as she was requested and took a sip. 'That's it,' she decided, firmly convinced. 'When can you start?'

# 7

## A LITTLE EXPERIMENT

Once she had absorbed the fantastic news that the accounts had been faked, Sheila couldn't wait to get back home to pass on the glad tidings to her mother. She was so excited she constantly exhorted Harry to go faster, until he was forced to calm her down in case there might be an accident.

'You don't understand,' she urged. 'Mummy's been going out of her mind worrying about it all, trying to keep the place tidy – she must be worn out with it all by now. I'll probably have to call the doctor. There you are.' She pointed dramatically at the front of the cottage. 'See, all the curtains are drawn, that means she's in bed, worn out by it all.'

When they burst in at the front door they found Mrs M sitting back comfortably, her feet up on the sofa, happily sipping her favourite cocoa.

'Mummy, are you all right? What's happened?'

'You may well ask,' she replied complacently. 'Take a look for yourself. We've had a few changes here.'

'Good grief,' cried Harry, for the room was transformed. Gone were the saggy cushions and the battered looking table and chairs. Instead, a beautifully clean background was revealed, complete with highly polished furnishings and not a speck of dust to be seen.

'Who did all this?' squeaked Sheila, dumbfounded.

'My new housekeeper,' purred Mrs M. 'He came in answer to my ad. I don't know how he did it, but I was so pleased, I gave him the rest of the day off.'

At her words, Prince started racing around the room, barking excitedly.

'I think I might know who it could be,' said Harry hastily, alerted by the dog's antics. 'But before we go any further, may I introduce you to Mary, who has something to tell you. I think you'll be pleased to hear what she has to say.'

'Yes, Mummy, you'll never guess,' burst out Sheila, diverted from the spectacle. 'This is Trustworthy's secretary, who says he's nothing but a fraud.'

Her words had an electrifying effect. Mrs M sent her cup of cocoa flying as she sprang to her feet with a cry of delight. 'I knew it, at last he's been found out. This calls for a celebration. Get a bottle and glasses and tell me all about it.'

In the midst of all the congratulations, Harry quietly let Prince outside to do his wee-wees and issued a warning and a stern rebuke. 'Just watch it, Prince. I know what you're thinking and I don't know how your valet, Jazz found out, but keep it to yourself. Nobody will believe it and even if they did, it would give Mrs M a heart attack. Okay?'

Prince wagged his tail and did a little dance. 'I knew he wouldn't let me down. I can't wait to see him again.'

'I dare say,' cautioned Harry, 'but we've still got that inspector breathing down our necks, and we haven't proven anything yet. I need to see the sergeant to ensure Mary doesn't come to any harm meanwhile.'

'You'd better make sure Sheila doesn't get the wrong idea.'

'That's just what I was thinking,' agreed Harry with a sigh. 'Come on, let's get it over.'

But to his surprise all was harmony inside. Sheila was fussing over Mary like a mother hen with a new chick, and Mrs M sat there smiling benevolently, as if everything was back to normal. Not wishing to spoil the mood of the moment, Harry asked his landlady if he could have a word with the new housekeeper, before leaving in the morning to check with Sergeant Matthews.

Receiving her assurance he retired to bed, happy that events seemed to be moving in the right direction.

His feeling of contentment was reinforced next morning after a discreet tap on the door heralded the entrance of the new housekeeper, who enquired if sir would like a cup of tea or coffee.

Braced by his presence, Harry opted for tea and drank it down quickly, anticipating the feverish welcome that Prince was bound to provide when he woke up.

'I have taken the liberty of running you a bath, sir, if that is what you require,' enquired the new housekeeper sedately. 'And breakfast is ready, whenever you wish.'

'Right, oh and before I forget, a quick word with you before I go.'

'Sir?'

Harry hesitated, then put the question bluntly. 'Jazz, and I assume that is who you are. How far would you go to protect the family, while I'm not here?'

Prince's valet gave an indulgent smile. 'I fancy that would be the postman at the door. If you would care to watch, while I conduct a little experiment?

'Yes, can I help you?' he enquired, opening the door. As the postman reached out with his delivery, Jazz clicked his fingers, freezing the postman's movements on the spot and turning him into a statue. He clicked his fingers again and the postman came to life. After handing over the letters, he touched his hat and departed happily, leaving an awed silence behind him.

'I see what you mean,' acknowledged Harry, deeply impressed.

'I have taken the liberty of placing your breakfast in the oven to keep warm while I acquaint his Highness about your intentions to visit Sergeant Matthews, sir.'

'How the devil did you know that?' Harry was mystified.

'Mrs Merton was good enough to inform me last night.' He coughed. 'I take it you do not intend to take his Highness with you at this stage?'

'No, you're darned right I don't,' said Harry with feeling. 'There's no knowing what his Highness might come out with. His presence would call for a lot of explaining, and I don't feel up to it just now.'

'Quite so, sir. If you will let me know when you wish to depart, I will summon a taxi.'

On his way, Harry toyed with the idea of trying to explain the sudden appearance of Jazz to anyone, but the very thought of what this might lead to made him feel dizzy. No, he would just stick to the facts and what Mary told him. Crossing his fingers, hoping that the inspector wouldn't stick his oar in, he tapped at the sergeant's door and poked his head in hopefully.

The sudden sight of the visitor waiting patiently for his friend to appear caused Harry to panic and he instinctively started to back out.

'Ah,' barked the visitor, 'Mr Bell, if I'm not mistaken, or should I say, Mr Smith? Don't just stand there with your mouth open, come in.'

Harry froze. 'Colonel Slaughter?' he ventured, remembering their earlier fraught encounter. 'I do apologise, I was looking for Sergeant Matthews. I didn't realise he had a visitor.'

'Nonsense, you're the very man I want to see.' The Colonel looked at his notes. 'What's all this nonsense about your landlady being under suspicion – she put me up at one time when I started out in my early days as a copper. Dammit, she wouldn't hurt a fly.'

Harry began to breathe a bit more freely. 'I'm glad you see it that way, sir. I know three witnesses who are willing to vouch for her, at the time in question. If you have a word with her daughter, she'll tell you the same, I'll stake my life on it.'

The Colonel shot him a quick glance. 'Like that, is it?' He chuckled, noting Harry's embarrassment. 'Let's get down to business. I suppose that latest inspector of mine has got the wrong end of the stick, as usual. Still, he's keen, I'll give him that. Now, what's all this about you working undercover?'

Harry drew a deep breath. 'I expect Sergeant Matthews will bring you up to date on that side of it, sir, but you might like to know that I've spoken to Trustworthy's secretary, and this is what she told me.'

He went on to explain that he had shown her the leaflet listing suspects that the police wanted to question. One of the suspects known as "M.T Banks" she recognised as being her late manager who was listed as a con man. The other, listed as Scarface Willie, and so on.

Listening with keen interest, the Colonel made some notes and seemed lost in thought for a moment. Recovering, he admitted with a sigh, 'Looks as if we've got off on the wrong foot on this case from the start. Your Uncle Ted was right about you all along. I should have followed up what he had to say in the first place. Incidentally, does this Mary of yours need police protection? Sounds to me if she might need it.'

Harry hurriedly vetoed the idea. The thought of trying to explain how he had first encountered Prince and everything that had since occurred made him shudder inwardly. 'I don't think that's necessary just yet, sir,' he cautioned. 'It might draw attention to her. I've left her in good hands,' he added convincingly.

'I suppose you're right, we don't want to give the opposition any ideas. So, what's our next move?'

Harry weighed up the pros and cons. 'It all depends on whether Trustworthy revealed my identity to the rest of the outfit before he disappeared. If he was... ahem... "seen to" before he had the chance to tell them, I might still get away with it.'

'That's taking an almighty risk,' objected the Colonel. 'Isn't it about time we had a word with this boss of yours to find out whether he is a genuine plainclothes man, or not? I don't seem to have any record of him. You might be walking into a trap.'

Harry faced up to the threat squarely. 'I don't want to risk it at this point, sir, in case we're barking up the wrong tree.' He pondered. 'If only we could be sure he's on our side.'

'I know, didn't Matthews arrange a contact for you, in case of emergencies – Rachel, someone or other? Wouldn't she know?'

Paling at the thought that Sheila might hear about it, Harry thought hurriedly. 'No, she was with me when Trustworthy was about to denounce me. It would put her at risk. Don't worry, sir, I'll stick with Smith as a cover for the time being. I'll keep in touch with Sergeant Matthews as a back-up, if that's all right with you.'

'I hope you're right,' acknowledged the Colonel dubiously. 'Leave it with me for now. I'm not at my desk at the moment, as you can see. I called in on my way to the office to see for myself how the staff are getting on.' He chuckled. 'Keeps them on their toes, they don't call me Slaughter for nothing. Well, off you go, Bell, I'll inform the sergeant about our discussion when he arrives. After that, l suppose I'd better inform the inspector, otherwise he'll get the wrong ideas again.'

To suggest that the inspector might get the wrong ideas was the understatement of the year. Directly he heard about the latest developments he dismissed them out of hand when his sergeant made the mistake of venturing an opinion.

'Wait and see?' he demanded. 'Is that all you can say, Winkle? When the answer's staring you in the face? They're all in it together. How that landlady managed to get off with the help of those witnesses I shall never know. In my opinion, she's sheltering that secretary of Trustworthy's to stop us getting at the truth. From now on, I want a full report of everyone who is seen to enter or leave that lodging house, understood?'

'Yes, sir,' said the sergeant hopefully, seeing an opportunity for promotion.

'And if you see anyone acting suspiciously at any time, I want them brought in for questioning, right away.'

'Yes, sir,' repeated the sergeant with slightly less enthusiasm, at the thought of all his precious free time vanishing up the chimney.


Meanwhile, reassured by the thought that Jazz was keeping guard against any intruders, Harry reported in at his office, waiting for the inevitable summons from his manager, Simon Shaw.

Questioned closely about his movements, he gave a straightforward account about the attack on the accountant, and that his disappearance was currently being investigated by the inspector in charge of the case, Chief Inspector Pain.

'Did Trustworthy say anything to you before the attack took place?' asked Shaw casually. 'Or mention anything unusual when he arrived?'

'No, sir,' replied Harry innocently, crossing his fingers behind his back. 'Was he expected to?'

'You quite sure about that?'

'Of course,' lied Harry, trying to sound convincing.

'No reason,' dismissed the other, changing the subject. 'I

hear that Mary, his secretary, is staying with you at the moment. Is that correct?'

Harry relaxed, feeling the worst part of the interrogation seemed to be over. 'Yes, she was so overcome by what happened, I thought the rest would do her good.' He added, 'We thought it would be better if she stayed with us to get over the shock and help her forget about it all.'

'Is she staying there permanently?'

'It's up to her, of course,' answered Harry innocently. 'The landlady has said she can stay as long as she likes, before she decides when it's time to get back to work.'

'Yes, that appears to be satisfactory. When she is better, we will have to find her a new position.' He sat up and shuffled a few papers together. 'Now, the more immediate question is, what do we have lined up for you to do in the meantime. Have you any suggestions, now that you have familiarised yourself with the situation, in view of the recent upheaval?'

Harry thought for a moment, wondering if this was a good opportunity of testing his manager's real identity. Taking a chance, he said impulsively, 'To tell you the truth, it's all been such a shock to the system, I find myself wondering who I am sometimes, and who everyone else is.'

Much to his disappointment, Shaw did not take the bait. 'Naturally, that is understandable, considering the circumstances.' Putting aside the notion for a moment, he said briskly, 'However, now that our accountant seems to have disappeared, perhaps you could cast your eye over the hotel accounts and see how it's getting on. Keep me posted if you discover anything suspicious. Take tomorrow off and think about it. We could, no doubt, arrange for Rachel to look after you again, when you get back.'

Accepting the offer of a break, Harry beat a hasty retreat before the manager had any more thoughts about engaging a secretary for him. Feeling elated at the unexpected freedom,

Harry decided to seek out the sergeant if he was free and bring him up to date with the latest developments.

Hearing about the meeting with Mary, the sergeant whistled with astonishment. 'She was able to identify him from that leaflet I gave you as Banks, our con man, was she? That's amazing. I don't know why we didn't think of that before. I can't say I noticed anything from that leaflet that would have helped to establish Trustworthy's real identity, but being his secretary no doubt that would have helped. It's a pity we don't have a record of his fingerprints, unless,' he thought for a moment, 'he left some on those accounts of his. I'll get my secretary to check that up.'

'Do we have any from when he was arrested under the name of Banks?'

'That's a thought. I'm not sure how long ago that was, but we'll follow it up. Thanks for reminding me.'

'What sort of a man was he, and how did you get on to him?'

The sergeant reflected. 'He was a devious character, slippery as an eel. It happened a few years ago, before I got my stripes. There was an elderly widow living in Tanfield and he persuaded her to let him look after her affairs. She'd been left a sizeable inheritance from a rich uncle which left her a sitting target. By the time her nephew got onto it, he'd spent most of her savings and it was too late to do anything to get it back. The nephew was so cut up about it, he challenged Banks and they had an almighty row, ending up with him being charged with fraud. Unfortunately, he managed to skip bail and disappeared. After that, nothing more was heard of the villain and we lost trace of him, until now.'

'What about Scarface Willie?'

'Ah, he was another shifty character. Always in gang fights, even at school, so I'm told, then he got mixed up with a bunch of drug dealers and got sliced up by a rival gang, hence his nickname. Finally, he ran out of luck after being convicted of assault and threatening a witness.'

'What happened to him?' Harry was curious. 'Was he the one Mary was talking about?'

'That's a good question. He also disappeared off our screen, so it would be interesting to find out if he's the same one she mentioned. If he was in touch with Trustworthy, he could be working for the same outfit.'

'I'd certainly like to meet up with him,' Harry said feelingly. 'It was his scar Mary was tracing out on my face when Sheila discovered us and got the wrong impression.'

The sergeant hid a smile. 'My, you do get around, don't you. All we need now is Butch Jones, what a scoop. You'd be able to collect a sizeable reward for that lot.'

'We don't seem to have anything on him, do we?' reflected Harry. 'He sounds a real tough nut, by his description.'

'He's in a different league altogether,' cautioned the sergeant. 'As you see, he's wanted for false identity and attempted murder, but that's only half of it. He's a nasty character, and since he's been around, he's acquired a notorious background that would have shamed any American gangster. I wouldn't be surprised if he'd been in touch with Trustworthy as well. If he has, you need to watch your step, or you could end up in a concrete overcoat.'

'That's assuming we can prove it,' replied Harry soberly. 'It looks as if they're all tied up with that PR company, and meanwhile we don't know what's happened to Trustworthy.'

'You've done far more than we ever expected,' counselled the sergeant. 'Who would have thought you would have got this far with only a couple of wanted notices to go by.'

'But how are we going to prove all this?' said Harry, frustrated. 'We don't know where Trustworthy's vanished to, and we haven't a clue which side Shaw is on. There are so many questions that remain unanswered, I feel like a blind man without his dog to guide him.'

'Don't be so down on yourself,' the sergeant encouraged, 'you've done a great job.' Seeing that Harry was not convinced, he came to a decision and opened up. 'I wasn't allowed to tell you this before, but we've had strict instructions about this case. It's not just a small-time affair we're up against here, but major league stuff, all very hush hush. I'd better explain. A special unit was set up to deal with it at national level, otherwise it would have been handled in the normal way by our Chief Constable. But as his was a new appointment it was put on hold to see how he shaped up. When you tried to arrest him by mistake that time, he wasn't very pleased and they weren't sure how he was going to handle it. They didn't think much of our bossy inspector either, so the Super got landed with it and I was assigned to help him. As soon you got involved with that fake audit account of Trustworthy's and his link with that phoney PR outfit, I was told to contact you and enlist your support. So now you know.'

'That's something, I suppose,' accepted Harry, pondering over the new information. 'But how does Shaw fit into it and what am I supposed to do?'

'You'll have to know, sooner or later,' revealed the sergeant thumbing through his files. 'Here you are, these are his details. Major Simon Shaw, ex SAS, seconded for special duties, currently in charge of the operation.'

'So, he *is* on our side,' breathed Harry, relieved. 'Thank goodness that's cleared up.'

'I was not supposed to tell you that, so mind you keep it to yourself. Now the cat's out of the bag, I'd be in dead trouble if it gets around.'

'Don't worry, Sarg, it gives me something to go on. I wonder what brought him into it.' He reflected. 'So the Super is involved as well, is he?' He followed the idea in his mind. 'I suppose the answer could be to do with that hotel business. Now I've got those account details that the inspector doesn't seem to want to know about, that's something I could follow up. Only make sure you don't land me with another secretary like that Rachel again. Perhaps you could find me a more elderly type next time. Let me know who it is in advance, if possible.'

'I'll see what I can do, but I can't promise anything.' The sergeant sounded doubtful. 'Your boss Shaw shuts up like a clam if I ask him anything. That's what comes of serving in the SAS, I suppose. Anyway, be very careful how you deal with him, now you know. It might put all our lives in danger, if you put a foot wrong.'

'Yes.' Harry considered. 'I'd better limit our meetings from now on.' He debated whether to let his friend in on his secret about Prince, but on reflection he decided that would be asking too much for anyone to believe out of the blue, even at this stage.

He cleared his throat and decided to drop a hint to prepare his friend. 'Don't be surprised if you hear something unusual though, in the next few days.'

After he departed, the sergeant pondered on his remark. 'I wonder what he could mean by that. It couldn't get more unusual than what I've just told him.'

Feeling he knew at least one of the answers, Harry decided to treat himself to a taxi and returned home to ponder his next move.

Greeting him on his arrival, Jazz assured him that all was well. 'Except for the two gentlemen watching the premises, sir.'

Intrigued, Harry peered out of the window under cover of the curtain and recognised the figure of Sergeant Winkle hovering in the background. 'Looks as if that inspector is keeping an eye on us, I wonder why?'

'I gather from His Highness that the inspector is not entirely convinced about Mrs Merton's innocence, sir.'

'The man's an idiot.'

'Yes, I fear so, sir.'

'Hello, is that the phone? No, I'll take it, Jazz. Get someone to pop Prince out to do his wee-wees while I answer it, will you?'

As he picked up the phone, he heard Mary's voice calling out, 'Don't worry, I'll do that. He probably needs a bit of exercise. Come along with me, darling. What a sweet little lamb. This way.'

Reassured, Harry asked the caller, 'Who's that?'

At the sound of Sergeant Matthew's voice, he sat down and listened. 'What's that, they've found a body? Sorry, I can't hear you very well, there's an awful racket going on outside. I'll have to ring you back, someone's calling for me.' He put down the phone reluctantly. 'Yes, what is it,' he called out, 'I was on an important phone call.'

The face of Jazz, appeared at the doorway, looking distinctively ruffled. 'I'm sorry to bother you, sir, but it's the police. I understand they've just arrested Miss Mary and his Highness for loitering and causing an obstruction, and have decided to take them in for questioning.' Seeing the shock on Harry's face, he added, 'I gather the sergeant also took exception to being attacked and was bitten on the leg, sir.'

## 8

# WATCHING AS INSTRUCTED

'It's that darned inspector again, I expect,' responded Harry automatically, his mind still reeling, following the sergeant's report of a body.

'I wouldn't know, sir. May I ask what you would advise?'

'What? Oh, I see what you mean. We'd better get down to the police station right away and see if we can sort it out.'

When they arrived, Harry saw with a sinking heart a car pulling up and the inspector climbing out, with a barely concealed look of triumph on his face.

'Oh, it's you, is it.' He snorted. 'I might have guessed you'd be involved. I hear your hound has made an unwarranted attack on my sergeant. What have you got to say about it, eh?'

'We've only just arrived, Inspector,' Harry defended himself quickly. 'I've yet to hear from Mary what happened.'

'I can tell you what happened,' interrupted the inspector rudely. 'My sergeant has told me all about it. He was interrogating your young lady who was loitering in the vicinity, when that dog of yours launched an unprovoked attack and injured him. I'm taking them in for questioning and charging. Vicious brute, he needs putting down, if I have anything to do with it.'

There was a slight cough and a respectful voice was heard in the background. Harry stopped what he was going to say and listened to the housekeeper, who he knew would be more diplomatic.

'If I might make a suggestion, Inspector,' Jazz broke in smoothly. 'Perhaps if we were to hear from the young lady concerned, it might throw some light on the matter.'

'No time for that,' snapped the inspector. 'I've already told Winkle to take her statement.'

'I rather fancy the reporter who's joined us would rather hear it now,' insisted Jazz firmly.

'What reporter?' asked Harry, puzzled, looking around without seeing anybody.

'Yes, what reporter?' snapped the inspector curtly. 'I can't see anybody.'

Just as he spoke, a form materialised out of the gloom, complete with a flashlight camera already poised.

Before Harry could work out what was happening, they were interrupted by a voice sounding like a reporter eagerly asking questions.

'No comment. A statement will be made after the suspect is charged,' snapped the inspector furiously.

'Perhaps sir's solicitor would also be interested to hear the substance of the charge?' suggested Jazz.

Harry was about to question his remark when another form started materialising, wearing a gown. Choking back a feeling of disbelief at the sight of the apparition, Harry woke up, seeing Jazz's hand in it, and gave his full support. 'Quite right, I would like to hear Mary's account before you start arresting anybody, and so would my solicitor.'

'Oh, all right,' said the inspector huffily. 'We'll go inside and my sergeant will explain.'

Once inside, the sergeant took the hint and started. 'Following your instruction, sir, I watched the young lady and the h'animal loitering outside the said premises acting suspiciously with intent and when I attempted to apprehend them, the dorg attacked me in a vicious manner and inflicted multiple cuts and contusions, sir.'

'Right, satisfied? Prepare the charge, Sergeant.'

'Wait a minute, Inspector,' argued Harry, incensed at the accusation. 'You've got it all wrong. For a start, Mary is staying with us, and all she was doing was taking Prince out for a walk. She offered to do it while I was answering the phone.'

'She was definitely loitering, sir,' objected the sergeant. 'I was watching as instructed.'

'Never mind that,' fumed the inspector, turning to Harry. 'Is there anyone here who can collaborate your version of events?'

'Of course,' agreed Harry. 'If we go back to my lodgings, it can be sorted out.'

On their return, he led them inside. 'Mrs Merton,' he called out, 'can we have a word?'

As she appeared all flustered from the kitchen, he introduced the two officers and invited, 'Perhaps you would like to ask her yourself, Inspector.'

'What is it, Master Harry... I mean Tom,' inquired Mrs M getting flustered. 'I was just starting supper.'

'Sorry to bother you, Mrs M. The inspector would like to ask you a few questions.'

'Pardon me, madam,' he said pompously. 'Do you know this young lady?'

'What a daft question,' she said impatiently, wiping her hands on her apron. 'Of course I know her. It's Miss Mary, she's staying with us as a guest. If it wasn't for her, I'd still be in trouble with that wretched accountant, bless her heart.'

'We don't need to go into that,' said Harry hastily, knowing the inspector's suspicions. 'I gather the inspector would like to ask you about her recent movements while she's been staying with us.'

'Well, she's only been here five minutes, but she's a great help. Always asking what she can do. She even offered to take Prince out to do his wee wees while the master was on the phone just now. She's a real pet.'

'There's still that violent assault, sir,' reminded the sergeant. 'Left me with multiple contusions like.'

'I was only protecting her from that idiot policeman,' piped up an unexpected voice.

'What did you say?' demanded the inspector, taken aback, looking from Mary to Prince in a dazed fashion, completely confused.

'If I might offer a solution,' suggested Jazz, catching on. 'I fancy that might be my master, ahem doing one of his impressions to lighten the proceedings. He is so good,' he added with a discreet smile, 'I sometimes wonder whether he should be on the stage as a ventriloquist.' Getting back to the matter in hand, he suggested gently, 'I hope that answers your questions, Inspector. As my master will, I am sure, point out, Prince was only doing his duty as a faithful pet by protecting his mistress under trying circumstances when the sergeant threatened to arrest her.'

He added apologetically, 'However, if you still insist on taking the matter any further, I rather think my master will be left with no alternative other than consulting our solicitor, which would I imagine end up in court, resulting in punitive damages for wrongful arrest, isn't that so, sir?'

'Too right,' said Harry warmly. 'And an apology to Mary wouldn't come amiss.'

'After hearing the explanations, I don't think we need to take this any further,' decided the inspector hastily. 'I accept that a mistake has been made,' directing a nasty look at his sergeant as he spoke, 'and I hope the young lady will overlook our actions and any upset this may have caused.'

'Good, that's settled.' Harry heaved a sigh of relief. 'Then we can assume that there won't be any further intrusions of this nature in future?'

'Not unless the law requires it,' agreed the inspector stiffly. 'Come along, Sergeant, I want to have a few words with you.'

As they departed, Prince added his own verdict. 'He's the one who should be put down.'

In his haste to get away before any further slights were made on his authority, the inspector pretended not to hear the last remark, but his sergeant was left nursing his pride over the incident. To add insult to injury, directly they got out of earshot, the inspector lost no time in blaming him for the whole event, patently ignoring the fact that the sergeant was following his instructions in the first place.

Vowing revenge, Sergeant Winkle put through an anonymous call to the local paper as soon as he was dismissed. Covering up the mouthpiece with his handkerchief, he whispered hoarsely, 'Is that the Courier news desk? I want to make an anonymous complaint about a vicious assault...'


Relieved that the confrontation with the inspector appeared to have been resolved, Harry immediately tried to get back to Sergeant Matthews, only to be told he had left for the night.

Anxious to find out what the earlier call mentioning a body was all about, he realised that an early visit to Police HQ in the morning was his next priority. Before doing so, he had to be sure that Mary had recovered from her ordeal with the inspector and was not faced with any more risks.

Mrs M soon put his mind to rest. 'Poor love, she was so worked up over that sergeant trying to arrest her that I fed her and sent her off to bed straight away. I knew you wouldn't mind.'

'No, of course not, Mrs M. That's exactly what I would have suggested. D'you think she'll be all right?'

'Yes, she's fine. I just went up to make sure and she's sleeping like an angel, poor darling. You've got that dog of yours to thank for that.'

'Why, what's he done?' asked Harry, hoping Prince hadn't blotted his copybook again.

'He told that sergeant where to get off, didn't he. Stood right in front of Miss Mary and wouldn't let anyone go near her, until that silly sergeant tried to arrest her.'

'And he bit him,' reminded Harry. 'He shouldn't have done that.'

'Serve him right,' sniffed Mrs M. 'That'll teach him, trying to make out she was loitering and then having the cheek to lay his hands on her, what do you expect? He's a little hero in my book. Fussed over her afterwards like a little gentleman. He worships her, anyone could see that. I gave him a special bowl of treats as a thank you, he deserved it.'

'Then I won't disturb her,' decided Harry. 'Better make sure she has a good lie-in tomorrow and see to it she doesn't get disturbed; I've got to go out tomorrow to see Sergeant Matthews about something that's cropped up.'

'I'll do my best, Master Harry, but there's no holding her now, with that Prince she's taken a fancy to. She told me she can't wait to take him out again for walkies.'

Harry swallowed. 'That'll have to wait. Look, Mrs M, on no account let Mary out while I'm away tomorrow. Now that she knows about that accountant, her life might well be in danger until we have proved it. To be on the safe side, I'll take Prince with me.'

'Oh dear, she will be disappointed. Now why don't you sit down while I serve up supper and see if I can persuade that housekeeper to have something to eat as well.'

'That's just what I was going to suggest,' approved Harry. 'I want to have a word with him as well.'

.  .  .

'So, you see, Jazz, it's vital that I take his Highness with me tomorrow, otherwise Mary might not be able to resist the temptation and take him out again. Apparently, she's taken quite a shine to him.'

'I quite understand, sir. Will you be wanting a taxi?'

'I'll see if I can cadge a life with Freddie. I seem to remember it's his day off and I'm not sure of my movements.'

'Very good, sir.'

After finishing off his supper quickly, in his haste to contact Freddie, Harry wished he'd accepted the offer that he'd airily declined. It wasn't until late in the evening that he was able to make contact and found it meant he had to make an early start when his friend would be free.

Feeling rather tired after being stuck on the phone for so long, Harry decided to pack it in and catch up on what Prince had been up to, if he was still awake, knowing his snoozing habits.

When he got to the bedroom, Prince was not only awake but crooning to himself in a lovesick way that Harry found rather touching.

'Well, Prince, how are you?' he enquired, interested to hear both sides of the story. 'Feeling better, after that attack on the sergeant. What did he do to deserve that?'

'How can you treat it so casually, when he had the effrontery to molest that angel?' was the indignant response he received.

'Got it bad, have you?' asked Harry lightly. 'Don't say you're smitten at last, after fending off all those attractive females who must have been after you in Palmesia, with all your dazzling prospects.'

Prince shuddered. 'Don't remind me, they were nothing to me. Mary is a goddess, my first and only true love. I would do anything for her, you name it.'

'And how are you going to go about it?' asked Harry

patiently, trying to be realistic. 'Get Jazz to take the spell off you, just like that? I thought you told me Jazz wouldn't be able to do anything about turning you back, until you had carried out some sort of special act of helping others.'

'I didn't have any option, did I?' said Prince bitterly. 'It was either that or end up in the dungeon, if my cousin had anything to do with it.'

'Well, now's your chance,' said Harry wearily. 'Help me out solving my investigation and you might be lucky. Fat chance I've got at the moment, with the prospect of another dead body to deal with. I'm turning in, we've got an early start in the morning if I want to cadge that lift with Freddie.' He lifted a warning hand. 'And you don't think I'm going to leave you behind for Mary to take you walkies, do you? And put her at risk with that inspector breathing down my neck with another loitering charge? Forget it, you're coming with me.'

Lifting the still protesting Prince into the back of Freddie's car the next morning, Harry found himself going over the whole saga of the previous day's events before his friend would be satisfied.

'Ah, that would account for that local news item I heard before I picked you up,' Freddie said with an understanding grin. 'Listen to this. He twiddled a few knobs on the car radio. The result was spluttering sounds mingled with the blast of an impatient driver behind, wanting to get past. After a while, he switched it off, defeated.

'Steady on,' urged Harry, 'or you'll have us in a ditch.'

'Never mind, I can give you the gist of it,' promised his friend, slowing down. 'Apparently, they had an anonymous call about a cop being savaged by a dog as he was about to make an arrest of someone for loitering. Sounded a bit peeved about it.'

'The idiot got it all wrong,' hooted a voice from the back. 'She was taking me for a walk.'

This time, Freddie managed to bring the car to a shuddering halt without causing an accident, just missing a telegraph pole in the process. 'By gum, he's at it again,' he uttered, awestruck. 'And I swear you didn't move your lips.'

'I told you, it's just a knack,' repeated Harry hastily.

'And that caller said something about a ventriloquist getting in on the act,' recalled his friend wonderingly. 'You do get around, don't you.'

'Let's hope that blasted inspector keeps to his word and doesn't take it any further,' said Harry, without thinking. 'I've got enough problems as it is, now they've found a body.'

# 9

## WHAT BODY?

The remark was so unexpected that Freddie forgot what he was going to ask next and responded feebly, 'Body – what body?'

'It's to do with an undercover job that Sergeant Matthews has got me involved in,' admitted Harry, wishing he hadn't mentioned it. Then noticing the look of bewilderment on his friend's face, he took pity and relented. 'It's all very hush hush, so don't bandy it around. He's got me to investigate a company with a shady record, hoping I'll find out enough to put them behind bars. They've already come up with a missing body, and they want me to look into it.'

'Gosh, you don't do anything by halves, do you,' exclaimed Freddie enviously, 'and there was I thinking you might be going on the stage, with that act of yours.'

'No such luck.' Harry sighed. 'I sometimes wish I was back on the beat like you.'

'Well, let me know if there's anything I can do to help.'

Stirred by the immediate offer, Harry thought it over. 'Thanks, mate. You never know, I might take you up on that. At the moment, I know as much as you do about this latest development, so I'll have to wait and see what the sergeant has to say. And here we are,' he added as they drew up outside Police HQ.

'You won't forget to ring me, will you,' reminded Freddie. 'I'm free after my shift in a couple of hours. And don't forget your dog.'

'As if I could. Time for your wee wees, Prince,' he commanded as he got out. 'Not another word, while I'm with the Sarg.'

'What a funny thing to say,' remarked Freddie to himself as he pulled away. 'Anyone would think his dog was the ventriloquist.'


'Ah, Harry,' welcomed the sergeant, 'I've been trying to get in touch with you. Did you get my message about the body that's turned up?'

'Yes, what's it all about? I couldn't get back to you yesterday after that dratted inspector tried to arrest us. He gave up in the end when we threatened him with a solicitor.'

'I know, I saw something about it in the newspaper,' sympathised the sergeant. 'What happened?'

'Apparently the Chief Inspector got his sergeant to arrest anyone he thought was acting suspiciously at my lodgings, just as I got your report of a body being found. But what's that all about?'

The sergeant pulled a paper towards him. 'We had a call from the local police yesterday. A farmer out Spenfield way was driving his tractor on one of his fields overlooking a quarry when he caught sight of a burnt-out wreck of a vehicle below and reported it to the local police. When they inspected it, they found what was left of a charred body inside. Here is a picture they've just sent over.' He handed it over. 'Not a pretty sight, is it?'

'Any chance of identifying the victim?' asked Harry hopefully.

'Still awaiting lab reports.' Sergeant Matthews looked at him keenly. 'You thinking what I'm thinking?'

'Trustworthy?'

'Could be, but it's too early to say.'

'What about fingerprints?'

'No chance, burnt to a frazzle.'

Harry rubbed his chin thoughtfully. 'So where do we go from here?'

'The only thing we're going on is the hope that an analysis of some of the fibres left on the body will give us a clue; what sort of clothes he was wearing, that sort of thing. Other than that, the only thing they can be sure of was that it was done fairly recently. The farmer confirmed the wreck wasn't there last week.'

'Any reports of missing people?'

'Not so far. That's another funny thing,' he mused. 'Spenfield is mainly a farming community. If anyone local went missing, it would soon get around. Also, there've been no reports of any missing vehicles,' he added, anticipating the next question.

'But this is crazy,' Harry objected. 'People don't disappear just like that.'

'They do if someone is covering up,' Sergeant Matthews pointed out.

'Can we get any of the locals to look at the corpse and see if they recognise him?'

'When they heard about the state he was in, there was a concerted rush for the exit,' replied the Sarg glumly.

'What about that PR firm of Trustworthy's. Can't you get anyone from there to take a look?'

'Well, there is that secretary of his,' began the Sergeant. 'But I understand she's still recovering from that business with your dog being arrested.'

Harry grimaced. 'I wouldn't advise asking her at the moment, unless it was absolutely necessary.'

However, when he phoned up to enquire about her progress, he discovered she was up and about and gamely insisted on viewing the remains.

Afterwards, fighting off a feeling of nausea at the sight of the body in front of them, she came out with an unexpected remark. 'No, I don't think it could be my boss, he always insisted on wearing brown suede shoes, whatever the weather. He wouldn't be seen dead in those.' She pointed at the heavy boots on display. 'Those aren't brown suede, what's left of them, are they?' Realising what she'd said, she covered her mouth in confusion.

'That's sorted one thing out,' decided the sergeant, after they had absorbed the implications. 'If that lass is right and it isn't Trustworthy, it means you won't have to be called as a witness at the inquest now if there is one, whenever that is. So, you can continue using your alias, after all.'

'That's true,' acknowledged Harry thankfully. 'But more importantly at the moment, I think Mary could do with a strong cup of tea, after going through that ordeal.'

After ensuring that she had not suffered unduly from the gruesome spectacle, he pondered on the fate of the corpse with his friend, as they parted. 'I wonder if he turns out to be another of those suspects who have disappeared. Perhaps I'll be able to find out tomorrow when I get back to work.'

But the news did not appear to have reached the office when he arrived. On the contrary, the staff at reception were poring over the report in the local newspaper about the inspector's failed attempts to make an arrest and giggling at the account of one of their own members of staff putting him off with impersonations as a ventriloquist.

Making the most of the distraction, Harry made for his office and, seeing that there was no secretary present to disturb him, began to look through the hotel files for anything that would help his investigation.

After an initial fruitless search, he was on the point of giving up when the phone rang. It was Alastair Brown's secretary, asking him to report to his office.

Feeling nervous, Harry sat on the edge of his chair going over in his mind what the likely topic would be. Was it to be about the body that had been found, and if so, would Brown be likely to admit it might one of the missing PR men?

One look at his face was enough to make him cross the forbidden subject off his list. The manager was looking too benign, almost avuncular, as he sat there comfortably straddling the chair.

'Now, Mr Smith, or can I call you, Tom?'

'Call me Tom, by all means.' Harry swallowed, taken aback by the sudden change in the manager's attitude, now almost like that of an uncle with his favourite nephew.

'Good. You are no doubt wondering why I have asked you in for a little chat.'

'No at all, sir,' denied Harry, thinking, perhaps it was about Trustworthy after all.

'Let me put you straight on one point, it's not about your work. I have had some splendid reports on your progress.'

'Glad to hear it, sir.' Despite the assurance, he remained tense, waiting for the question, about another body.

'No, what has concerned me is the spate of rumours that have been flying about recently. Have you been made aware of them at all?'

'No, sir,' answered Harry quickly, mentally urging the other to get on with it, so he could hear the worst, whatever it was.

'Well, I don't mind telling you, in confidence, of course...'

'Of course,' encouraged Harry, privately wondering when, and if, his superior was going to get to the point.

'The fact is.' Brown paused, then he began again. 'It has

been brought to my notice that a number of allegations have been circulating recently, involving members of my staff, that are entirely without foundation, I might add.'

'Naturally,' Harry encouraged.

'I'm glad you see it that way.' The other nodded, sitting back, gratified at the reaction. 'So, what is to be done about it?' Without waiting for an answer, he added, 'I pride myself that we have always been a happy ship, except for one or two minor hiccups.' He hurried on, not waiting to be challenged on the issue. 'So I have come to the conclusion that what we need is a diversion, something to help us relax and take our minds off things and make us count our blessings.'

He paused and flexed his fingers. 'And do you know the first thing that occurred to me?'

'No idea, sir,' answered Harry promptly.

'The one person I immediately thought of, was... you.'

'Me, sir?' echoed Harry blankly.

'Yes, you, Tom. It surprised me at first, but when I came across that report in the local paper about those impersonations, I knew it was the answer I was looking for.'

Before Harry could think of an excuse, the manager smote his desk enthusiastically. 'That's it. Don't you see, what we need is an event to take people's minds off everyday problems – entertainment, that's what we should go for, and you're just the man to help us.'

'But,' objected Harry, bewildered, 'what do you expect me to do?'

'I can see it now.' Brown waved his arms excitedly. 'It's coming up to Christmas, the timing couldn't be better. We'll take over the Globe Theatre in the High Street for a special performance. That should go down well locally, they'll be queuing up to see it. Let me see, we can start off with a dance routine.' He coughed. 'I'm sure Mayor Fox could introduce us to enough young ladies to fill the bill; then one or two solo acts, a singer, what's her name, Sue someone or other...'

Harry almost ventured "Saucy Sue," but thought better of it.

'...and that juggling act my nephew was anxious to promote. I can think of dozens of others, then the grand finale, your ventriloquist act, I can see it all now, it will bring the house down.'

*I will certainly do that*, agreed Harry to himself, trying to imagine attempting to coach Prince doing anything, without ending up giving the game away. 'But, sir,' he argued, 'it would involve my dog, Prince in a kind of double act. I don't think that would go down at all well.'

'Nonsense,' overruled Brown cheerfully. 'It would be the climax to the whole show, according to this report in the paper.'

'If you say so,' accepted Harry, privately horrified at the thought.

'While you're working out a routine, why don't you familiarise yourself with some of our other activities that you can promote. Let me see, what about the hotel account. I don't think you've met the owner yet, Alderman Fox, our mayor, have you?'

Harry winced, remembering his last encounter with the mayor's previous girlfriend, Saucy Sue. 'No, I haven't had that pleasure.'

'I see from his schedule that he's away at the moment, but it will give you the opportunity to check whether everything is running smoothly, as it should be, in his absence. You'll be surprised at the number of celebrities we have staying there at the moment. We've even got an Earl, what do you think of that?'

'I'm impressed,' said Harry politely.

'You have to remember to address him as Mr. Smith,' advised his manager. 'He likes to travel incognito because he's always being asked to invest in something or another because of his money. He's got stacks of it and gets tired of being pestered, so he tells me.' Amused at the idea, he exclaimed, 'Why, that's your name as well, what a coincidence. It will give you something to talk about when you meet him.'

'I don't expect he will want to be disturbed, if he feels like that,' protested Harry. He was not in a hurry to get involved with any of the tenants at this stage. All he wanted to do was to go through the accounts and see what he needed to investigate.

'Nonsense. No time like the present,' boomed the other with relish, heaving himself up with some difficulty from his chair. 'Come along, why don't we pop over to his hotel and look him up? I usually call in to see him about this time. I'm looking forward to this.'

Arriving at the hotel and taking the lift to the top floor he tapped discreetly at a door and beamed as it was opened by a valet. 'Morning, Manners, is your master in?'

'Good morning, sir. I'll just see if he is free.'

He disappeared from view and a few minutes later returned and ushered them in. 'If you would step this way, sir.'

Opening a door at the end of a short corridor, he announced, 'Mr Brown and a guest, sir.'

A tall, elderly figure uncoiled himself from an armchair by a bay window overlooking the hotel grounds and got up to greet them.

'Ah, Alastair, good of you to look in. I see you've brought a friend to relieve the monotony. Good show.'

'Yes, let me introduce my colleague, Mr Tom Smith. I thought it might amuse you to meet another of your namesakes.'

'What, I don't believe it.' The Earl beamed. 'How do you do, Tom, if I may I call you that?' He held out his hand and said frankly, 'Look here, I won't beat about the bush, but whenever someone uses that surname they're usually trying to sell me something, but I gather that's not the case. Will you join me in a drink?'

Harry hesitated. 'Would you think me rude if I had a lager?'

'Excellent, a man after my own heart.' He pressed a bell and the valet appeared, as if by magic. 'Manners! A lager for our guest and I think I'll have the same. Your usual, Alastair?'

As the drinks were handed out, their host raised his glass. 'Here's to you, Tom. Now, is this a leg pull on account of the name we share, or is there something I should know about?' He shot a quick look at Alastair. 'It's not about Geoffrey, is it. He's okay, is he?'

'No, he's quite all right,' assured Alastair. 'I saw him down in the bar with some friends earlier on.'

'Good.' Their host offered Harry an explanation. 'Just checking. My grandson has been under the weather recently.' He sighed. 'Got us all a bit worried for a time. His wife passed away a few months ago after a long illness and he's finding it difficult to get over it, as we all are.'

Harry put his drink down hastily and expressed his sympathy. 'I'm sorry, I didn't realise. Perhaps we should leave this to another time.' He shot a questioning look at his manager.

'No, don't think about it,' insisted their host, pressing Harry's arm. 'Now, tell me all about yourself, Tom. What are you doing in this part of the world? Have you known Alastair long, or is it just a visit?'

Seeing there was no escape, Harry cast a covert glance at his manager for a nod of approval before launching into a quick resume of his role in the company, getting ready to depart as soon as an opportunity arose.

Much to his chagrin, he was almost finished when his manager glanced at his watch and got to his feet, apologising profusely. 'Is that the time, I've just remembered I was supposed to ring someone ten minutes ago. If you'll both excuse me.' As Harry half rose to join him, he was waved down.

'No, don't get up. I don't want to spoil things just as you're getting to know one another. Tell him about our plans for the show, Tom. Don't forget to mention our special finale.'

'Yes, don't hurry away, my boy,' insisted their host. 'This sounds interesting. What's it all about?'

Harry obediently explained the idea proposed by his manager to put on a special evening of variety acts at the local Globe Theatre at Christmas, ending up with some sort of ventriloquist act – as he put it, 'involving myself and my dog,' he ended up ruefully.

'Really? Have you done this sort of thing before?'

Harry tried to explain and got so mixed up his host pressed another drink on him, then another until he began to lose all track of time and found himself relaxing and listening to his host fondly reminiscing about his own past. As the light was by then beginning to fade, the valet appeared like a genie and began to close the curtains and busied himself switching on some extra lights.

Breaking off, his host insisted that Harry should stay for supper and to his surprise he found himself accepting. The food when it came was so tasty that he expressed his appreciation and his host leaned across impulsively. 'Let's forget all this Mr Smith nonsense. I expect Alastair's told you I'm an Earl for my sins, but I can't help that. Just call me William, Tom.'

Harry almost choked over his food at the unexpected familiarity and was touched by the friendly gesture. 'I'd like that, um William,' he responded.

It was very much later that he reluctantly got to his feet and made his excuses. 'I feel it's about time I went. I hope I haven't outstayed my welcome, but I really enjoyed meeting you, sir.'

'Don't call me sir, or I'll never invite you again. It's William, don't forget.'

As they shook hands, his host exclaimed in parting, 'It's extraordinary, I don't know why, but I have the strangest feeling we've met before somewhere, at some point in our lives. Isn't it odd. I tell you what,' he said, 'why don't you come to lunch tomorrow and meet my grandson, Geoffrey, and we can swap some more tales. He's got a better memory than me. How about that, say about one o'clock?'

Much to his surprise, Harry agreed. All the way back to his digs he had the strange feeling that their paths had crossed before.

# 10

## ALL HE WANTED TO KNOW

On time, he presented himself at the Earl's door the next day, just in time to see someone leaving. As the man passed, furtively stuffing a bag into his pocket, Harry caught sight of a tell-tale scar on the side of his face, half hidden by a scarf and a hat tilted at a jaunty angle, partially concealing his features.

In that split-second encounter, Harry stored a mental image of the stranger, and as soon as the other had passed he bent down out of curiosity to investigate a few white grains that had escaped from the stranger's bag and lay scattered on the floor. A quick sniff told him all he wanted to know. Snow! Someone was into drugs.

His training enabled him to identify it instantly. Many the time he'd pulled in a drug runner only to be vilified by the indignant parents, who when confronted were unable to face up to the truth. Who could it be? He refused to believe it could be the Earl, he didn't look the type. In that case, it had to be Manners, the valet, or Geoffrey.

His mind raced at the possibilities. There was only one way to find out. He tapped at the door and was rewarded with the sight of Manners who appeared after a slight delay, looking unlike his usual urbane self.

'Please step this way, sir. I will ascertain if his Lordship is free.' Returning after a few minutes, he ushered Harry into the sitting room. 'If you would care to take a seat, his Lordship will be along directly. Meanwhile, can I offer you a drink?'

Intrigued at the reason for the hold-up, Harry decided to put the question of drugs to one side for the moment until a more suitable occasion arose and politely declined, deciding to wait until his host appeared.

After a few more minutes, the Earl hurried in looking distinctly ruffled, apologising for the delay. 'So glad you could make it, Tom.' He smoothed back his hair and straightened his jacket. 'Must apologise, Geoffrey will be with us in a moment, he's just getting over one of his turns. Manners, get me a whiskey, will you?' He emptied his glass in one swallow and remembered his guest. 'How about you, Tom? Still sticking to your lager, or can I offer you something a bit stronger?'

'Lager would do me fine,' acknowledged Harry quickly, then casually to avoid arousing suspicion, said, 'Gets these turns often, does he?'

'Yes, every now and then. Nothing to worry about, so he tells me. Ah, here he is. Geoffrey, come and say hello to Alastair's friend, Tom. He's been looking forward to meeting you.'

A casually dressed young man ambled into the room, blinking at the light. 'Do we need all those lights on, Grampa,' he complained. 'You know I can't stand it. Ah, that's better,' he said as the valet switched off some of the overhead lights. 'How d'you do? I'm Geoffrey,' he managed, slurring some of his words. 'Most people call me, Geoff.'

In that instant, Harry knew who was the culprit. Extending a welcome hand, he found himself half assisting the young man to the nearest armchair. 'Hi, I'm glad to meet you, Geoff. I'm

Tom. Let me help you, I hear you've been under the weather recently. My dad passed away not all that long ago,' he said, managing to sound convincing, 'so I know how you must feel.'

'There you are,' encouraged the Earl. 'Nothing to be ashamed of, Geoff. We've all been there, one time or another.'

Geoff brushed away a tear impatiently and Harry noticed his puffy eyes and the slight tremor in his hands. 'Nothing I can't handle,' he insisted defiantly. 'I just need a pick-up now and then to help me. Thank you, Manners, a whiskey for me, if you please.'

Getting a nod from the Earl, Manners turned away and poured a small measure into a glass and discreetly added some water before handing it over.

Gulping it down, Geoffrey threw the empty glass down on the tray disgustedly. 'Even the whiskey tastes like water these days.'

In an attempt to steer the conversation onto safer grounds, Harry latched onto his previous remark, idly reflecting, 'Talking of water, I wonder what recreational facilities are available around here these days. Does the hotel have its own swimming pool, for instance?'

'Fat chance,' snorted Geoffrey. 'The nearest one is miles away.'

'Pity that,' broke in the Earl enthusiastically. 'Geoff here was top of his class at swimming at school, weren't you, my boy. Shame you didn't keep it up.'

'Beryl wasn't very keen on it,' admitted Geoffrey, his eyes brimming with tears at the thought of it.

Harry mentally kicked himself for arousing old memories, but Geoffrey carried on regardless, lighting up a cigarette and stubbing it out a few minutes later, before lighting another one, as he recalled painful episodes from the past. 'There were a lot of things she wasn't keen on, like taking the dog for a walk. I had to get rid of him in the end, poor old Muffin, it broke my heart, that did.'

'That's enough of that,' interrupted the Earl hastily. 'I'm sure Tom doesn't want to hear about all that. I tell you what, why don't we have a game of cards? Fancy a round of whist, anyone?'

Geoffrey flung his half-smoked cigarette away tearfully. 'You don't understand, any of you. All you can think of is playing games, as if nothing has happened, now Beryl is gone. I can't stand it!'

He lurched to his feet and stood there, swaying. Harry started to get up, ready to assist but their host was there before him, taking Geoffrey by the arm and steering him out of the room, making soothing remarks as he held on. 'Steady on, my boy, you're upsetting our guest. Why don't you have a quiet lie down and we'll talk about it in the morning.'

As soon as they were out of the room, Harry caught hold of the valet as he was leaving and spoke urgently. 'Wait. How long has he been going on like this?'

The valet drew himself up respectfully. 'I don't think it's my place to offer an opinion, sir.'

'You can trust me, Manners.' Harry was quietly insistent. 'He's on drugs, isn't he. I passed the dealer coming in. Cocaine, isn't it, he left some of it on the mat. I recognised the symptoms.'

Manners went pale at the thought. 'It's more than my job's worth, sir...'

'Don't worry, I won't report it, I promise, but you've got to help me. How long has he been using them?'

The valet regarded him searchingly before coming to a decision. 'As long as you promise, sir – about three months or so. I couldn't inform his Lordship, sir, it would break his heart. I tried to remonstrate with the young master, but he wouldn't listen to me.'

'Right, as I thought. When you've got a moment, I want to know how he got hooked. He needs to go into rehab, but that's another story. Meanwhile, leave it with me and I'll see what we can do. Mum's the word. Look out, he's coming back.' He raised his voice.

'I say Manners, any chance of a lager? I seem to have developed a bit of a thirst, it's all that talk of swimming pools, I expect.'

'Yes, sir, certainly.'

Overhearing Harry's last remark, the Earl seized on it thankfully. 'That's what started off Geoff just now, all that talk about swimming pools. Brought back old memories. That business with Beryl has preyed on his mind. Bad show, that,' he said gruffly, 'but it's time he learned to live with it. I've had to, dammit. Beryl was my favourite as well, don't forget.' He pulled himself together. 'We can't all go on like that. If we did, we'd end up in the looney bin.'

He laughed shortly, determined to banish any further gloomy remarks from the conversation, and turning to Harry raised his glass in a salute. 'But I don't mind admitting, Geoff bucked up when he heard you were coming, Tom. It's what he needs, someone his own age to talk to, to take his mind off things. I say,' he said, struck by a sudden thought, 'I don't suppose you could find the time to pop in, now and then, to keep his spirits up? No,' he immediately apologised, 'I shouldn't have asked, I've got no right to, when I'm sure you must have lots of other business commitments to think about.'

Harry jumped at the opportunity to find out more about the drugs problem and tried not to sound too eager. 'No, as a matter of fact, I've got nothing on at the moment, only a few boring accounts to follow up at some point. I'd like that very much.'

'Well in that case,' replied the Earl, inspired, 'why don't you stay here for a few days? That's if the idea appeals to you,' he added hopefully. 'We'd love to have you and Geoff would be delighted. Manners will look after you, you've only got to say the word.'

Harry finished off his drink and stood up, pleased with the way things were going. 'Come to think of it, that sounds rather a good idea, if you could put up with me. In fact, it would answer all my immediate problems. I was wondering where to put up, while I'm on my present assignment.'

'I am sure Geoff would provide all your essentials, to save you going back,' suggested the Earl tactfully. 'He's about your size.'

'That's very kind of you,' acknowledged Harry hastily, 'but I'd better let my landlady know where I'm planning to stay, otherwise she will wonder what's happened to me. She's a dear old soul, but likes to worry, gives her something to do, bless her heart.'

'Of course,' agreed the Earl sympathetically. 'Just give me a bell when to expect you.'

Waving goodbye, Harry waited until he was back on the ground floor at the hotel entrance before reaching for the nearest phone. Checking his watch, he put a call through to the sergeant, hoping to catch him before he left for the day. Turning away from the reception desk so that he could not be overheard, he spoke in a soft voice, asking to be connected.

Hearing the sergeant's voice bellowing 'Who's that?' down the line, he decided on second thoughts to wait until he got back to his digs before leaving a message, and called for a taxi.

When he arrived home, however, he was met with disturbing news that took his mind off his immediate problems. Answering the door, Jazz drew him aside and broke the news that Mary was being followed.

'Is she all right?' demanded Harry, alarmed. 'Where is she?'

After reassuring his master that the young lady in question

was safe and unharmed, Jazz explained, 'It appears that Miss Mary became aware that she was being followed when she took some letters to be posted. She very sensibly reported the matter to Mrs Merton and myself when she returned, and I have been keeping the intruder under observation since it happened. Miss Mary didn't seem to be unduly affected by the unwelcome attention, but I persuaded her to retire early and have a complete rest after her experience, sir.'

'Thank you, Jazz. It's a good thing you were here to look after her. It couldn't have happened at a worse time, as far as I'm concerned,' he admitted. Feeling an urge to confide, he confessed, 'I'm right in the middle of an important assignment and need to get back to where I'm staying, after I've spoken to Sergeant Matthews about it.' He hesitated. 'It might mean I'll be away for a few days or so.'

'You need have no concerns on that matter, sir,' Jazz assured him. 'I will make sure that Miss Mary does not leave the premises while you are away, and only then if I accompany her personally.'

'That's a relief. Look, I'll have a word with Mrs M about it after I've contacted Sergeant Matthews and brought him up to date.'

Leaving Jazz to explain to the others, Harry made for the phone. He was about to pick up the receiver when he noticed a message had been left.

It was a recorded message from the sergeant. *'Heard you were trying to contact me, Harry. I'll be in my office after ten tomorrow, after I've followed up a report on Trustworthy. See you then, hopefully.'*

Harry left a brief message to confirm and went to join the others where he gave a guarded report on his latest investigations, not wishing to alarm them about the dangers of drug dealing. It was enough, he hoped, to satisfy Mrs M, but not Sheila who seemed to revert to her earlier suspicions about his past actions which he promptly denied, hoping it would satisfy her.

He was just congratulating himself on escaping any further questions when Prince, waking up and overhearing the exchange, piped up innocently, 'What about that Rachel, she was a hot one.'

Thinking it was Harry who spoke, the mere mention of her name was enough to revive bitter memories, and despite his entreaties Sheila stormed out of the room and rushed upstairs, refusing to speak to anyone. Alarmed at the outburst, Harry followed her up to her room and tapped on the door, begging to be let in. 'Sheila, darling, that's all in the past. It was all a silly mistake, nothing to get upset about.' But she was not to be drawn, and all he could hear were muffled sobs, so he reluctantly gave up.

Next morning, after making sure that Prince was quite happy to remain behind to worship Mary, and there were no signs of any intruders for her to worry about, Harry left at last with a heavy heart, wondering sadly if he had done the right thing by not staying and trying to persuade Sheila, knowing how stubborn she was once she got an idea in her head. He could only hope that if he was successful in solving the drug threat, it might make her relent.

On hearing his news, Sergeant Matthews was not slow to show his feelings and whistled in surprise at the latest news. 'As if we don't have enough on our plate – drugs, I ask you. No wonder, if Scarface is involved, it used to be meat and drink with him. With one of the tenants in the mayor's hotel, you say? I'd better let the chief know.'

Five minutes later, he put the phone down and picked up his file. 'He wants to see us right away. I'll take the notes I've made.'

. . .

'As you see, sir,' he finished, after bringing his superior up to date, 'it looks as if we've got something to hang it on at last.'

Colonel Slaughter scratched his chin reflectively. 'So, it's drugs at the back of it? What a vile trade. Still, if what our young friend here says is true, it may be what we're looking for.' He gave Harry a searching glance. 'You do know what you're letting yourself in for, don't you. It could be dangerous. Are you prepared to take the risk?'

Harry shrugged off the dangers and nodded. 'I've seen what it does to people, first hand. If I can do anything to put a stop to it, I'm willing to deal with any dangers that may arise.'

'Good lad. Then go ahead and keep us informed. I don't think it would be appropriate to bring Inspector Pain in at this stage, until we've got something for him to follow up.'

Both Harry and the sergeant gave a sigh of relief at the thought, and the Colonel smiled with understanding. 'Just so, we'll leave it at that for the time being. Any questions? By the way, Matthews, in view of your close involvement in this case and the extra responsibility, I've decided to promote you to Detective Sergeant. Don't let me down.'

'No, sir. Thank you, sir.'

The delighted newly appointed Det. Sgt Matthews saluted and escorted Harry out. After recovering from the idea of his sudden rise in rank, he warned his young friend, 'Don't forget to keep in touch. If I know anything about Scarface Willie and the rest of that mob, they won't take kindly to you treading on their toes.'

'Don't worry, and congratulations, Jimmy, if I may call you that, you'll be the first to know if I come up with anything.'

Feeling happier knowing he had the full support of both the Chief and his old friend behind him, Harry wasted no more time before getting in touch with the Earl and accepting his invitation for lunch and to stay on for a few days.

The valet's honest face lit up when he answered the door. 'I am so glad you were able to come, sir. His Lordship will be pleased to see you, I am sure. Master Geoffrey is lying down at the moment.' He lowered his voice. 'I'm afraid his moods are getting more unpredictable since you left, but I'm sure he will be glad to see you when he recovers.'

'Has he had any more supplies?' asked Harry quickly, hearing the Earl approaching.

'One this morning, I regret, sir. He usually calls mid-afternoon when his Lordship is resting so I can deal with him, but this is something new. I tried to get rid of him, but Master Geoffrey insisted.'

'Never mind, it can't be helped. Ah, hello, sir, er William, good of you to put me up.'

'So glad you could make it, Tom, come in and make yourself at home. Manners will see to your things. Am I glad to see you, poor old Geoff is having one of his turns again, I'm afraid, but he'll be up shortly. Ah, excuse me, that's probably the golf club secretary.' He rubbed his hands in happy anticipation, as the telephone rang outside in the entrance. 'They called yesterday asking if I could make up a round this afternoon, I expect that's them again.'

After a few minutes, he popped his head around the door. 'Yes, as I thought. Ronnie, the man I usually partner, has gone down with flu and they're in a bit of a stew. I say, now you're here, do you mind awfully if I desert you for a couple of hours? It's a frightfully important match, they tell me. Manners will look after you.'

'No, off you go,' replied Harry, glad of the opportunity to

find out how the Earl's grandson was coping with his drug habit.

When Geoffrey eventually appeared, he was clearly on the defensive and greeted Harry warmly like an old friend. 'So glad to see someone on my side, Tom, isn't it,' he said thickly, leaning across confidentially. 'They didn't want me to have my medicine. Pour me a whiskey, there's a good chap. Manners keeps on spiking my drinks, don't trust him. Had the cheek to try and stop my delivery.'

Harry did as he was asked. If he was to gain Geoff's confidence he had to play along. Handing it over, he enquired sympathetically, 'Here you are. How're you feeling?'

'Don't ask,' said Geoff tossing it back. 'Thank the Lord you turned up.' His voice took on a self-pitying note. 'They're all against me, even Gramps. Pretending they care, it's all bunkum.' His voice started trembling. 'I've got nobody I can trust. You'll see I get my supply tomorrow, won't you, Tom, it makes me feel strong again, if only for a little while. It's the nights that get me down, when visions of Beryl come back to haunt me.' He grasped Harry's arm trustingly. 'Say you'll help me.'

'Of course.' Harry spoke reassuringly, privately shocked at the state Geoffrey was in. It was even worse than he expected. He released the other's hand and steered him to a settee. 'Now, take it easy, tell me how you've been getting on.'

Just as Geoffrey was about to launch into a garbled account of his troubles, there was a knock at the door and Manners appeared and coughed. 'Excuse me, sir. Would it be in order if I departed now, it is my afternoon off.'

Seizing the opportunity, Harry rose to detain him. 'Just a minute Manners, if I may have a quick word. Won't be a minute, Geoff.' He joined the valet in the hall and spoke urgently. 'Before you go, do you have a note of Geoffrey's doctor? I think I need to speak to him as soon as possible.' He lowered his voice. 'He's worse than I thought. What was that?' There was a sound of a sudden splintering crash in the room behind them. He hurried back to see Geoffrey jumping up and down on some golf clubs that the Earl had left behind.

'Quick, Manners, lend me a hand.' He could see that Geoffrey was caught up in some kind of inner conflict and was screaming, amid a meaningless babble of words. 'Quick, ring the doctor and tell him it's urgent, while I try to calm him down.'

'Yes, sir, can you manage?'

'I think so. Don't waste time.'

While Manners hurried off to do as he was bid, Harry grabbed Geoff's arm soothingly. 'Come and sit down while I get some of your pills – where are they?'

After a struggle, all the fight went out of the other quite suddenly and he allowed himself to be led to the settee where he collapsed, sobbing. 'He doesn't give a damn; all he thinks about is his blasted golf. What's that you said, my pills, where? In my bedroom, in the back of the w-wardrobe.'

Harry left hm trembling and went in search of the drugs, discovering a packet hidden in a bundle, wrapped up in an old vest in the back of the wardrobe as directed, with more scattered around the room. He was just debating how much it would be safe to give Geoffrey in his present condition when Manners returned, accompanied by the doctor.

'Doctor Cornish,' the worthy introduced himself breezily. 'Where's the patient? Hello, young man, I haven't seen you for a while. What was it last time, measles or something. What seems to be the trouble?'

As he was chatting, his disarming manner managed to put his patient at ease, allowing the doctor to quickly run through a series of checks, testing his patient's pulse and peering at Geoffrey's red-rimmed eyes with his torch, before examining the drugs that Harry found. He turned them over with a resigned shrug. 'Hm, who's been a naughty boy, eh?' Before Geoffrey could utter a protest, the doctor produced a syringe and plunged the needle in. 'That should keep him quiet for a while,' he said with satisfaction.

'That's all I can do at this stage,' he explained later, after Geoffrey had been put to bed. 'What he needs now is constant supervision to make sure he doesn't get back into his old habits. Meanwhile, I need to talk to his Lordship to decide what's best for him in the long run.'

'Rehab?' guessed Harry, from experience.

'It may come to that, judging by the drugs you've found and how long he's been taking them. But I need to discuss it with his Lordship and decide what to do in the more immediate future, like getting in a full-time nurse to look after him and seeing that he is kept properly sedated.'

'May I suggest that whatever you propose is broken to his Lordship gently,' suggested Manners respectfully. 'I rather think it will come as a shock to his Lordship.'

'That sounds like him now,' said Harry, as they heard a key turn in the lock. 'Will you tell him, or shall I?'

'I think it would be better if you break the news,' suggested the doctor diplomatically, 'and explain why you felt it necessary to call me. I will be happy to follow it up by giving my professional opinion as to what steps we need to take to deal with the situation.'

'Thank you *very* much,' commented Harry, heaving a sigh. 'At that rate, I may need one of those injections myself.'

As he stepped forward to do the dubious honours, he came face to face with the Earl who had just entered and was in the middle of a jaunty little dance to celebrate his latest golfing success. 'Would you believe it, we wiped the board with them. The best round I've had in years!'

'Congratulations,' Harry began tentatively. 'Glad to hear you've had a good morning.'

'Good morning? Where's Manners, tell him to bring out a bottle of the best. This calls for a celebration.'

'Before we do that, I think there is something you should know,' said Harry, wondering how to broach the subject. He hesitated, then took the plunge. 'I think you'd better sit down, sir. Geoff's had one of his turns.'

The Earl was not surprised. 'Not another one. Never mind, he'll soon buck up when he hears my latest news.'

'It's a bit more serious than that.' Harry took a deep breath. 'He's got it so bad, I had to call the doctor.'

'What the devil for? You've got no call to do that,' remonstrated the Earl, peeved at the thought that his authority was being questioned. It was at this point that Harry decided not to mince his words, but tell the truth. 'Geoffrey's on drugs,' he said bluntly, not beating about the bush. 'He's been taking them for over three months or so, Manners tells me.'

'Drugs?' the Earl looked at him blankly. 'In my house? Never, not Geoffrey, he's still suffering from the loss of his wife, nothing more.'

'If you don't believe me, have a word with your doctor. He's just examined Geoffrey and has given him a sedative. While you're at it, take a look in his bedroom, the place is full of the stuff.'

The Earl stood up undecided, clearly not convinced. 'I must see this for myself.'

Fifteen minutes later he was back again, looking haggard and distraught. 'How long has he been like this, and how did you find out?'

'It was finding traces of cocaine outside on the mat that aroused my suspicions,' Harry admitted, 'but as soon as I met Geoffrey, I knew. He had it written all over him.'

'Good grief, why didn't you tell me?'

'Because I knew you wouldn't believe me,' answered Harry truthfully.

'No, I suppose you're right.' The Earl buried his face in his hands. 'I've always worshiped my family, and in my eyes, they could never do anything wrong, until this. If only I hadn't agreed to enter that blasted golf tournament.'

Harry stirred, remembering his host hadn't been told about the accident with the golf clubs yet, and braced himself for the effect it would have, coming on top of his existing woes.

'Er, there is one other thing,' he mentioned casually. 'Geoffrey got rather excited when he heard where you were going, and seems to have had a bit of a mix up with one or two of your golf clubs.'

The Earl groaned. 'That's all I needed. Where are they, let me see.' He got up wearily and Harry took him to the lobby where Manners had stored the remnants. Taking one look at the shattered remains, the Earl collapsed on a stool and broke down.

Although he sympathised, Harry couldn't see what all the fuss was about. 'Never mind,' he encouraged. 'You can always get another set.'

'You don't understand,' the Earl said miserably. 'They're priceless, as far as I'm concerned. They're part of our family history.'

'What's so special about them?' Harry was mystified.

'They were my grandmother's favourite, she was potty about them. Look, she even had her initials engraved on the handle, Lady M.'

A nameless dread took hold of Harry. 'Did you say, Lady M?' He swallowed.

'Yes,' the Earl said. 'It stood for Lady Mary. What a tragedy that was, she was so full of life, so lovely, you can tell it from those old photos we treasured. And she goes and throws it all away, all because of a silly romantic love affair that never came to anything.'

'Why was that?' But Harry already knew the answer, and the Earl confirmed it.

'Because he wasn't one of us,' he admitted gruffly. 'Of course, we had to hush it up, after she died having his baby. See, she left this ring with his initials.'

'Don't tell me, I know,' said Harry with sudden certainty. 'It was R.B.'

'How on earth did you know that?' exclaimed the Earl, astonished.

'Because I think it was my grandad,' was the simple reply.

# 11

## IT TELLS THE WHOLE STORY

'Don't be silly, Tom, how can you possibly know that?' said the Earl, astonished.

The answer came unwillingly, and he admitted with a sigh, 'Because my grandfather was Richard Bell.'

The Earl was unconvinced. 'But there must be thousands of men with a name like that, talk sense.'

Seeing there was no alternative, Harry felt in his pocket and produced a worn and somewhat faded envelope. 'This was the last letter Dad left, I found it in his desk drawer after he died. It tells the whole story.'

Taking it mechanically, the Earl read the contents slowly and reread it the second time to make sure there was no mistake. As the words began to sink in, he looked up in sheer disbelief. 'You mean to say, you've been posing here as my guest and friend, when all the time...' Words failed him.

'I honestly didn't know about it for sure until you mentioned it just now,' said Harry defensively.

'But you already had the evidence, from this letter.' The Earl was fuming.

'I've been carrying that around with me, hoping one day I'd find the answer,' confessed Harry, 'and now I have. It's all come as a bit of a shock to me as well.'

'You can't expect me to welcome you with open arms, now you've told me.' The Earl drew himself up forbiddingly, remembering the family history.

Putting aside the past with an effort, and anxious not to lose touch with his only hope of tracking down the drug dealers, Harry decided to appeal to the Earl's dwindling good will. 'Don't you see, I had to accept your invite, to find out where the drugs were coming from.'

'Dammit, why should you be interested? You hardly know Geoffrey.' The Earl refused to be drawn.

It was no use, the time for concealment was over. 'Because I'm working under cover for the police.' It was out.

'Where's your proof?' demanded the other, unyielding in his attitude.

Harry hesitated, then remembered. 'Here's my old warrant card.' He fished out his battered identity pass.

The Earl inspected it and began to thaw. 'Hmm, I suppose that begins to put a different light on it.'

'If it wasn't for Manners, I would never have known about it and fetched the doctor in time,' added Harry persuasively.

'So, he was in it as well, was he? MANNERS! Where are you, confound it. Show yourself.'

A head appeared at the doorway. 'Sir?'

'Were you involved in this skulduggery?'

'Yes, sir. I considered it my duty to support Master Tom directly I appraised him as to the facts of the situation. If it hadn't been for his decisive action, I hesitate to predict what might have been the outcome for Master Geoffrey.'

'I see, so it was all my fault, for not seeing it coming.' He meditated for a moment, then made up his mind, at last half resigned to the situation. 'Right, what do you want me to do, if anything?'

'First of all, which is of the utmost importance, I want you to promise me that you will not disclose my true identity to anyone outside this room, in particular to anyone like Alastair from the office.'

'Agreed, he's a proper old blabbermouth, I grant you. But what's it got to do with his firm?'

Harry was non-committal. 'There is a connection, too long to explain at the moment, sir, but I assure you it's essential. If you have any doubts, I suggest you contact Detective Sergeant Matthews at Police HQ.'

'Right, I'll take your word for it. What's next?'

'That takes care of the security aspect,' Harry pointed out. 'What we need to do now is to make sure that whoever is supplying the drugs carries on normally, to avoid arousing any suspicion. That way, I will feel free to work out how to follow him when he calls, and find out where he comes from.'

'I'd like to wring the perisher's neck, but I suppose I see the sense in that.' His host breathed heavily. 'How d'you propose to do that?'

'To make sure we don't miss him, I'd like to stay here just one more night to be around directly he appears, if that's all right.'

The Earl nodded his agreement. 'Anything you say, as long as you catch the swine. And don't forget to let me know before you do anything.'

'If I might suggest a possible solution,' offered Manners, 'I did manage to find out that the caller makes a regular drop off at one of the other flats on the ground floor. I could ask the manservant there to let me know when he is due.'

Harry considered the idea and privately turned it down, deciding that the idea of involving strangers at this point might be too great a risk. Then a sudden idea struck him. The answer was staring him in the face. Why rely on a casual acquaintance when he had his own bodyguard – Prince, of course. Nobody would notice a pet dog following him and he would keep him informed of the latest developments.

'A good thought, Manners,' he said quickly. 'Get him to warn you, by all means. But as an added precaution, I think I'll try something else as well.' Turning to the Earl, he explained, 'If I may take up your offer, I'd like to stay overnight, but meanwhile, I must call the office with a sick excuse to stay away, in case it drags on a few days, and meanwhile pop back to my digs to sort something out.'

'Well, now that's settled, I'd better call the doctor and see if he's fixed me up with a nurse to look after Geoffrey,' announced the Earl, his mind occupied with problems closer to home. 'Oh, and while I'm at it, I'd better ring my golf secretary and explain about the clubs. See you later then.'


As soon as the coast was clear, Harry put a call through to Det. Sgt Matthews to bring him up to date with the situation and received an instant response.

'We'll follow this up and let you know when we've made contact,' he promised. 'Where will we get in touch with you, are you staying on at the same address?'

'Yes, just for tonight, as far as I know,' decided Harry. 'We're expecting Scarface to drop off his delivery some time tomorrow, so I've got to nip back to my digs to let them know I'm staying.'


Back at police HQ, as Det. Sgt Matthews replaced the phone, Chief Inspector Pain marched in and overheard the tail end of his conversation. 'What was that, something about a drug delivery? I expect you to keep me informed, Sergeant.'

After the detective sergeant reluctantly gave him the information, he said softly, 'So, that could be useful. Drugs, eh? I will get my man to follow that up.' He picked up the phone. 'Tell Winkle to report to me at my office – immediately.'

Once he got back among familiar surroundings, Harry wasted no time and sought out Prince. He found him devotedly listening to Mary as she went about helping Mrs M with her usual household tasks.

'If I may have your attention, Prince,' he demanded, extracting the worshiping animal from her presence. 'I have a little task that I hope will not over tax your abilities.'

'What's the catch?' asked Prince. 'Mary promised to read me a story.'

'I'm sure that can wait until another time,' said Harry, pulling him away to gain his attention. 'Now, you remember Jazz saying he might lift that spell on you, if you made an effort to help others? Now's your chance to do so.'

'What do I have to do?' asked Prince suspiciously.

'Simply nothing. Just sit there in a swanky hotel and look out for our old friend, Scarface.'

'Is that all?'

'Of course, nothing to it.' Harry stroked the dog's ears persuasively. 'Easy-peasy. Directly you see him, all you have to do is to ring me at reception, and I'll be waiting for him.'

'How do I do that?'

Harry quickly explained. 'There's an alert button at reception, I'll show you, that's connected to all the rooms in case of emergencies. You just have to press it, and I shall know it's you.'

Prince thought it over. 'Okay, but how long do I have to wait?'

'Only a few hours, you'll be surprised how quickly the time goes by.'

'What about food? I'll need to keep my strength up.'

'No problem. I'll leave you something in a basket by the entrance, and the clerk on the desk will bring you lashes of food whenever you want.'

'There must be a catch in it.' Prince was not convinced. 'But I'm blowed if I know what it is.'

'That's my boy. Now, as soon as I have had a word with the others, we'll go back and I'll get the valet to look after you.'

'Why can't I stay with you?'

'The Earl who owns the apartment is not used to having pets around the place, so we'll have to be a little careful. But don't worry, Manners, the valet will do anything for me at the moment, so everything will be hunky-dory, you'll see. I will go and have a word with the others,' he said lightly, hoping in his heart that Sheila would be in a better mood than his last visit.

To his disappointment, he found that Sheila was away, staying with a friend for a few days. Mrs M was not forthcoming about who this friend might be and was elusive on the subject, which made Harry more heartsick than ever, wondering whether she would ever forgive him. In the end, all he could do was to ask her to pass on his love and scribbled a hasty note for her, before returning to the Earl's apartment with Prince in tow to await events.

Much to his relief, he was not questioned about Prince's presence. The Earl was out at the golf club and Manners greeted the new arrival with his usual stately aplomb, and without any explanations he found an old and comfortable basket in the spare bedroom for Prince to sleep in, without attracting any attention.

In fact, Prince was so comfortable in his new surroundings, what with all the treats that the valet lavished on him, that Harry found it difficult to rouse him next morning and be greeted with any enthusiasm.

'What is it now?' He blinked languidly, pulling the rug back over his face. 'Do you know what the time is?'

'Wake up, sleepy head,' ordered Harry, 'time we got started.'

'Doing what? I was just having a lovely dream, about Mary.'

'No time for that, it's eight o'clock. On parade, I've got to smuggle you down to the reception desk, ready for action. The sergeant promised to keep watch, but we can't take chances. We don't know when Scarface will turn up, so we've got to be ready for him.'

Grumbling, Prince followed him out and into the lift. Emerging on the ground floor, Prince pulled on his lead.

'What's up now?'

'I want to do my wee wees.'

Having got that ritual out of the way, Harry led him to the reception desk and turned him over to the clerk on duty, the necessary instructions were given and a generous tip was handed over.

'Don't forget, give me a buzz on that emergency button behind the counter as soon as you see him, and don't let him out of your sight. I'll be waiting for him.' Satisfied he had made himself clear, Harry returned to the apartment and ordered his favourite snack, a plate of crumpets, and a cup of tea to wash it down.

Anxious to get started, he glanced at his watch from time to time, willing the drug dealer to turn up and get it all over. As the time dragged by, he became increasingly nervous, afraid that his plans were about to go up in smoke. Just as he was about to get up and investigate, the buzzer sounded, sudden and urgent.

'Here we go,' voiced Harry, relieved the waiting was over. Springing to his feet, he waited a few minutes until there was a knock at the door and he saw Scarface handing over a package to Manners and turn to leave.

Giving his quarry a moment to move on, he crept out and

followed him, only to find himself in a queue for the lift, led by Scarface with Sergeant Winkle and Prince following closely behind.

Harry swore to himself. Trust Winkle to turn up, making things more complicated. Must have been that idiot Inspector Pain, determined to get the credit to himself, and muck the whole thing up. He watched the procession come to a halt at the lift. As soon as the lift doors opened they all squeezed in, except for Prince who got chased out by Sergeant Winkle after recognising him from his previous encounter.

What was he to do? Picking up the indignant victim and hugging him closely to his chest, he asked Prince hastily, 'Which floor?'

'Fourth,' was the muffled answer.

'Quick, no time for the lift.' He rushed for the stairs, taking them two at a time. 'Where did they go?' he asked the astonished clerk who was passing.

'The manager's office. You can't go in there,' the clerk warned, 'that's private. There's a security man on guard to stop anyone, unless they have an appointment.'

'Isn't there any other way in?'

'Only a balcony, if you're an acrobat,' the other added smugly.

Harry thought swiftly. 'I don't suppose there's an empty flat available on this floor?'

The clerk hesitated. 'Only number 15, sir, that's next door. Are you interested in taking it, sir?' he asked, pulling out a set of keys.

'Yes, just for tonight. How much?' He picked up the keys offered, checking them over. 'What's this other one for?'

'Ah, that one opens the door onto the balcony. Security, you understand.'

'Quite. I think I'll check in now, if you don't mind.'

'Certainly, sir. Do you have any luggage? I'll call the porter.'

'No, I didn't have time to pack.'

'You will find a spare pair of pyjamas in the hall cupboard,' offered the clerk, seeing an opportunity to earn a tip.

'Thanks, I might do that.' He slipped some extra notes in the waiting hand.

'Thank you, sir. Pets are not usually allowed, but as this is an exceptional case, oh, thank you, sir. Much obliged.'

'Good thing he didn't have time to think up any more excuses, I'd have been skint,' admitted Harry to himself as he shut the door behind him and flopped down on the nearest settee to get his breath back. 'Now for the difficult part. Let's see what that balcony's like.' He heaved himself up and fished out the keys. As he unlocked the door onto the balcony, he mused, 'I wonder where the others have got to?'

Directly he poked his head out, he discovered the answer. The man from the other flat had disappeared, and the frustrated figure of Sergeant Winkle came into view on another balcony in the distance, waving his arms and hoping to attract attention.

'Good, that'll take care of him for a while,' decided Harry, picking up Prince and slipping a handheld miniature recorder in his pocket. 'Here goes...' Climbing over the handrail, he measured the distance to the next balcony and caught his breath at the sight of the perilous drop below. Praying silently, he steadied himself and got ready to launch himself across the gap. Handicapped with Prince in his arms, leaving only one arm free to deal with emergencies, he felt himself slipping and his foot got caught up between the railings. As he hung there, he felt something slip out of his pocket and disappear into the depths.

'Oh, blast.' In desperation, he reached out to get a better grip while he freed himself, but stumbled and twisted his ankle, gasping at the pain. Unable to make the jump, he managed to heave Prince over to the next balcony, telling him to listen in and report back on any conversations he could hear.

Left to his own devices, Prince crept across to the window and peered through a crack in the curtains. Although his view was limited, there was no mistaking the battered face of Scarface Willie facing him across a small table, and a twitching arm belonging to a fat man with his back to the window.

Despite the thickness of the glass, he could hear snatches of disjointed conversation that built up in bursts of frustrated anger.

'Gee, boss, why can't you pay me more, I've been working my socks off since we started this racket...'

'...Because the job's not worth it, I can get kids by the dozen to do your job...'

'...But you promised I'd be quids in when we started. I've got at least another dozen drops to do before lunch. It's not fair...'

'...You do as you're told, or you'll and up like Trustworthy, if I have anything to do with it...'

'...It's not on,' the other's voice rose in protest. 'You must be earning a bomb out of this, and all I get are peanuts. I can get a better rate down in the docks. If you don't up the ante, I'll call on my mates to see to you. Then you'll be sorry...'

The burly figure in front of the window half rose and thumped the table menacingly. 'Do that and you'll be out of business – I'll see to that.'

Prince listened, storing the outbursts in his mind, and hoping to remember it, or at least some of it, by the time his master returned.

Meanwhile, relieved of the extra burden, Harry used all his remaining strength to climb back into the room he left to recover, while he worked out some other way to get across.

After resting for a while and testing his foot on the floor to help ease the aches and pains, he got up and combed through the other rooms until he came across a stepladder, used for decorating judging by the liberal splashes of dried paint in places. Feeling more confident, he hoisted it up and carried it out onto the balcony and placed it in position so that it lay across the two opposite handrails. Taking care to make as little noise as possible, he crawled slowly across the improvised gangway to join Prince waiting on the other side.

'What's going on?' he whispered, as soon as he landed and crouched down.

Prince made his report, clearly frustrated. 'I couldn't follow it properly. The curtains were closed, but I caught a glimpse of Scarface talking to a big fat man with his back towards us. He was complaining about not getting a rise in his pay and was told he wasn't worth it. They were getting quite worked up about it and the fat man was furious. He said something about ending up like Trustworthy, if he didn't watch his step.'

'Did you recognise the other man?'

'No, never seen him before.'

'Right, I'll try opening the door to see if we can hear anything.' He slid the key in and gently eased the door open a fraction.

As they leaned forward to listen, a thud occurred behind them that provoked an immediate reaction. There was a gasp from inside the room and the curtain was ripped aside and a face peered out, revealing the outraged face of Alderman Fox.

'Who the devil are you?' At his words, there was a flurry of movement behind the curtain, and the next moment the room was deserted and empty.

'Now see what you've done,' whispered Harry, mistaking the reason for the interruption. He fumbled in his pocket, found it empty and groaned. 'And just as I was hoping to catch them at it, I've gone and dropped my recorder! Bang goes my proof. That's all I need. That blasted inspector will never believe us now.'

As if to confirm it, the unmistakable figure of Sergeant Winkle appeared behind them and a hand tapped him on the shoulder.

'May I ask what you are doing, loitering with intent on this balcony in a highly suspicious manner?'

## 12

# REBELLION IN THE RANKS

'Ah, hello, Sergeant,' said Harry, taken aback. 'What are you doing here?'

'I might well ask you the same question, sir. This does not appear to be your balcony. Is the owner aware of this unwarranted intrusion on his premises?'

'No, he certainly is not,' snapped the owner, emerging from the window. 'How the devil did you get in and what do you mean by it?'

'Well, I er...' Stumped for a moment, Harry caught sight of Prince looking up at him hopefully and had a sudden inspiration. 'I came over to er um rescue my dog. Naturally I would do, when he...ah was in – distress, if you know what I mean...' Gaining confidence, he blurted out. 'Well, you would, wouldn't you in my position, it's only natural, after all.'

'Dammed if I see it. And who are you?' the owner demanded turning to the sergeant.

Hiding his annoyance at missing Scarface and fearful of what the inspector would say when he found out, Sergeant Winkle decided to appeal to the wrathful occupier. 'If you will allow me, sir, I will escort the intruder to the station for further questioning. Leave it to me.'

He waved at the open window, hoping in doing so he might discover any traces of the meeting he suspected had taken place, but found the room empty, much to his disappointment.

'This way,' fumed the alderman, standing aside reluctantly. 'I insist that you let me know about the results of your investigation after this gross intrusion.'

'You will be kept fully informed,' promised the sergeant, keeping his fingers crossed, relieved that his presence on the balcony had not been questioned. He hoped his actions would be enough to satisfy his inspector.

As it happened, all was quiet when they got back to Police HQ. The Chief Constable was attending a family wedding and the inspector had been called out in his absence to handle a disputed road accident that left him in a foul mood, and he was itching to take it out on someone. He was not in the best of spirits when he discovered his sergeant had got tired of waiting for him and was filling in time happily eating a double decker sandwich and downing a pint of beer.

Flinging his door open, he accidentally knocked the sergeant off his chair, sending the beer flying and soaking most of the files lying on his desk.

'What the devil do you think you're doing,' he yelled at the unfortunate sergeant. 'I thought you were supposed to be out hunting that blasted drug dealer, Scarface!'

'I was, I was,' yelped Sergeant Winkle, dabbing at his tunic frantically.

'Well? Did you nab him? What have you done with him?'

'Well, it was like this,' the sergeant began. 'It was all a bit of a rush, like, what with all the others involved...'

'What others? I told you not to tell anyone.'

'I didn't, I didn't, but word got around. It was like there was this queue, in a manner of speaking...'

'A queue? How many were there. For heaven's sake, it was supposed to be hush, hush. Who were they?'

'There were two or three people waiting in the lift, as we got there, then Scarface, then a scruffy dog...'

At that point, memory returned. 'It looked just like that brute that confronted me when I was on duty as instructed on a previous occasion, when he attacked me in a vicious manner, inflicting multiple cuts and contusions...'

'Never mind all that, who else was there?'

'Ah, well there was that there dorg, I've seen before, if you remember, sir.'

'Forget all that,' bawled the inspector, losing his temper. 'What happened next. Did you see where Scarface went?'

The sergeant shuffled his feet. 'When we got to the fourth floor, the accused pressed the bell and we all got out and then...'

'Then what, spit it out, man.'

His sergeant coughed. 'Well, it all got a bit mixed up after that. Scarface took it in his head to accuse one of the gentlemen in the lift of following him and there was a punch up and he fell down.'

'Who did?'

'The gentleman I was talking about, the one in the lift.'

'And what happened to Scarface, you dolt.'

'Oh, him. He took off and bolted down the corridor while I was helping this other one up.'

'Never mind the man who fell down,' screamed the inspector. 'Where did Scarface go?'

'I chased after him and sees a door open round the corner, and I dived in, but found it wasn't him, after all.'

'Give me strength. So, after all that, you're telling me you lost him.'

'Oh, no, sir. When I looked out on the balcony, I see'd him on another balcony, miles away.'

The inspector took a deep breath, trying to remain calm. 'I see, so you gave up. Well you'd better make out your report while I try to explain your bumbling to the Chief Constable.'

'Oh, but you haven't heard what happened next, sir.'

'Don't tell me, you discovered him in a cracker,' croaked the inspector, reaching wearily for the nearest chair to give him strength.

'No, so, it was like this. Wot I done was to count the number of balconies and worked out which one he was on, and there he was.'

'Scarface?' gasped the inspector weakly.

'No,' Sergeant Winkle announced triumphantly. 'That Harry Bell fella, the one you didn't like. He was after Scarface as well, I found out.'

Fighting to overcome his jealousy, the inspector managed to ask the question, 'What was he doing there?'

'He was keeping watch outside the mayor's place, hoping to hear what was a going on.'

'And did he?'

'He didn't let on. But old Foxy came out, all furious like, just as he was listening at the window.'

'Did he find out what was going on?'

'No, I heard him say he'd lost something, so he didn't get the proof he needed.'

'Idiot, I can't trust you to do anything.' Thinking it over, he told himself with satisfaction, *That's spoilt that wretched amateur's little game, he'll get it in the neck when he tries to explain that lot to the Chief. There's still a chance I might catch the blighters, after all.*

But Harry had other things on his mind. Foremost among these was what he was going to do with Prince while he was answering the summons to HQ.

Luckily, he found an ally in the Chief's secretary, who had always longed for a dog of her own, but had the same problem of where to leave it while she was working. On seeing Prince, all her motherly instincts came to the fore and she rushed forward ready to help.

Scooping up Prince in her arms, she cooed over him lovingly. 'Come to Mummy, darling, I'll look after you. If you're a good boy, I'll find you a nice biscuit to keep you going, and I expect you need to go for wee-wees, bless you.'

Relieved that his immediate problem appeared to be solved, Harry bent down and left strict instructions to the contented animal that on no account was he to utter a word to anyone, otherwise he would be in the soup.

But when the Chief Constable did return, the last thing he had on his mind was Prince's behaviour. It so happened he was in a jovial mood after attending a wedding. It transpired that it wasn't just a friend's wedding, but his cousin, who had recently been appointed to the post of Deputy Commissioner at Scotland Yard.

It wasn't only that snippet of good news that bucked him up. It was the fact that during the conversation, his cousin had tipped him the wink that as a result he was himself a strong contender for a much sought after position in the same department. If that happened, he was set up until retirement. So, he was inclined to be lenient and dismissive when hearing of Harry's unfortunate experience.

'It could happen to anyone,' he told his secretary. 'I remember the time when I was just starting off, you'd never believe what I had to put up with. There was this awkward inspector who would never listen to anything I had to say. He even had the cheek to stop my week-end pass, just because...' But his reminiscences were cut short by the appearance of Harry being ushered in. 'Ah, there you are, my boy. I hear you've had a spot of bad luck. What's it all about?'

Feeling apprehensive, Harry was about to launch into his tale when he was interrupted.

'Hang on,' decided Colonel Slaughter. 'Let's get Det. Sergeant Matthews to join us since he's involved in the same case.'

Hearing the tale unfold, his sergeant backed up Harry's account out of loyalty. 'Too bad he didn't get a chance to record the meeting. So, the mayor is the one we're after. The problem is, how are we going to prove it?'

The Chief Constable turned to Harry. 'Remind me, what exactly did Scarface say to the alderman that got him so wound up. That might give us a clue.'

Harry tried to recall the details of the conversation that Prince had passed on. 'It sounded as if he was complaining about not getting a rise in his commission for handing out the drugs and was told in no uncertain manner he wasn't worth it. They were getting quite worked up about it, in fact, and the mayor was getting furious at him. He said something about his boss dealing with him like Trustworthy, if he didn't watch his step.'

'Did he, by Jove,' commented the Chief thoughtfully. 'It sounds as if he might have known something about Trustworthy's disappearance. I wonder what he had in mind.'

'Trustworthy, eh? I'd give anything to know about that conversation with the mayor,' agreed the Det. Sgt darkly, thinking of the dead end they'd reached on the case they had almost given up pursuing.

As it so happened, the alderman turned out to be more concerned about how Scarface's threats were likely to affect his love life than anything else.

'Blast the man. He knows I'm dependent on him to pay for

my expenses. I'd be lost without Lulu, not to mention Fifi and Mimi and the rest of them.'

He was aghast at the hideous picture that presented itself, as images of his curvaceous lovers floated past in his mind. He thumbed through his bank statements to get at the facts. At a pinch, he could just about manage without Mimi, but the prospect of losing Fifi and Lulu as well made him shudder. He couldn't bear to imagine what life would be like without them, especially Gloria. What the devil was he to do?'

The same thought was echoing in the minds of his lovers, only from a different perspective.

'Did you see the look he gave Gloria, when she told him about it? If Scarface doesn't get a rise we'll soon be out of a job as well,' complained Lulu.

'And I'll be one of the first to go,' pointed out Mimi, as she removed her tattered tights. 'He thinks I've got nothing else to do but mend my undies.'

'I agree,' said Fifi, adjusting her bra. 'I think it's about time we put our rates up, that would teach him a lesson. He thinks he's getting us for next to nothing.'

'I'm with you there,' snorted Gloria. 'I could do with a bit of time off. If we go on like this, I'll lose all my tan, not to mention anything else. Let's face it, girls. The only way we can do that is to make him cough up. I don't know how old Scarface manages, running around like he does, peddling his drugs. It's a wonder the rossers don't scoop him in, at this rate.'

'Now you're talking,' enthused Lulu. 'Why don't we call a meeting about it. What say you, girls?'

'I'm all for it,' whooped Fifi. 'Let's down tools and call a vote.'

'Hear, hear!'

Taking command, Lulu summed up their feelings. 'As I see it, it's time he realised we're not here to be pushed around like a lot of old tarts. We have our rights, like anyone else.'

'You've said it, gal.'

'It's time we stopped fooling around and told him where he gets off. I vote we give him an ultimatum, like any other respected union in the situation. What d'you say. Am I right?'

'We're with you all the way.'

'Either he ups our rates by twenty percent, or I propose we go on strike. Is it agreed?'

'Twenty percent nothing,' piped up Gloria. 'What's wrong with thirty percent?'

'Or even forty?'

'Don't let's quibble about it. Make it fifty!'

'Carried unanimously,' declared Lulu to applause. 'Eat your heart out, Foxy.'

'Who's going to tell him?' asked Mimi, after a pause. They glanced at each other hopefully, then Gloria came up with an answer.

'Why not Scarface, he can be our spokesman. He's got as much to lose as any of us.'


When he was made aware of their decision, Scarface paled at the idea as, much as he was in favour, after all the risks he had undertaken the prospect of leading the rebellion was unnerving. Then, fortified by the excuse he had been given, he reached for the phone and started dialling.

To say that the Alderman was upset by the ultimatum would barely begin to express his feelings. He was so incensed by the demand he almost suffered a heart attack, so great was his rage.

'Fifty percent?' he choked, loosening his collar. 'Where d'you think I can get that sort of money. You must be mad!'

When he got his breath back, he gasped desperately, thinking of all the pleasures he would lose. 'Can't we agree on some sort of... compromise?'

'Such as?'

He made an attempt. 'Would they accept, say twenty?'

'You must be joking,' retorted Scarface, thinking of his cut.

'Well, twenty-five...I mean thirty...'

'Not a hope.'

'Thirty-five and that's my limit,' was the feverish reply.

For an answer, Scarface slammed the phone down in disgust.

The hapless mayor juggled with the receiver and phoned back. 'All right, but make it forty and that's my limit.'

'I'll try,' was the discouraging reply, 'but don't bank on it.'

A few minutes later he was back. 'It's no use, it's fifty or nothing.'

'Ah, this will ruin me! Tell them it's impossible.'

Back came a tempting offer. 'They said they'd throw in a free shower, if you agree.'

His eyes glistened. 'With the orange syringe as well?'

'Think again,' reported Scarface after checking. 'They said, "And what about the greengage?"'

He caved in. 'Yes, all right, dammit, you're on.'

Sunk in gloom, the alderman weighed up his prospects now they had settled the matter. How was he going to afford his new expenses. There was only one thing for it – he would have to increase the price of the drugs and to hell with it. He dismissed the anguish it would cause the victims. They had no alternative if they wanted their fix. *We can't all be winners,* he smirked, justifying his position. This meant calling for a meeting with Scarface to work out the next step as soon as possible. He would have to be careful it didn't come to the ears of that meddlesome intruder, whoever he was.

· · ·

Back at Police HQ, they were still going over the problem without coming to any conclusions when the inspector burst in, visibly excited at his news and expecting congratulations. 'Excuse the interruption, sir, but I thought you ought to know that a report has just come in that Scarface is doing his rounds again...'

'That's nothing new,' interrupted Colonel Slaughter irritably, annoyed at his officious tone. 'We know about that. What we need is proof.'

'But you don't understand,' insisted the other. 'One of them has been heard to say he's desperate and can't afford it any more – they say he's doubled his rates.'

'What?' broke in Harry excitedly. 'That's what Scarface was going on about when I listened in.'

'That's all very well, but is he willing to sign a statement?' The Chief Constable was not impressed.

The inspector halted in his tracks and puffed out his chest in complete assurance. 'Leave it to me, sir. I'll pull one of them in and force it out of him. Don't worry, I'll see to it. I'll get my Sergeant Winkle on it, he'll soon sort it out, never fear.'

After he had left, bristling with his own importance, his superior snorted. 'Fathead. They'll close up like a clam, scared stiff that Scarface will set the boys on them. I know his sort.'

'And he'll be expecting someone to trail him again. So where does that leave us?' reflected Dt. Sergeant Matthews gloomily.

'Come on, cheer up, men,' urged the Chief. 'What do you think, Harry, you've been closer than any of us to what's been going on. What do you suggest, any ideas?'

Harry racked his brains for a possible solution. He was just about to give up when a sudden idea struck him. 'I've just remembered, sir. I know this may sound idiotic, but if you recall, I was asked by Alastair Brown, head of recruitment at that dodgy company I've been investigating, to put on a variety act at the Globe Theatre in the High Street shortly, that our friend Alderman Fox will be organising.'

'How does that help us?' asked Colonel Slaughter mystified.

'He seems to think my efforts at putting on an amateur ventriloquist act might amuse the audience,' offered Harry helpfully.

'I don't see it,' replied the other, looking baffled.

'The mayor is bound to be in the front row, seeing as how he organised it.'

'And?'

'If I make it sound like my dog, Prince, starts asking him some awkward questions about his activities, it might catch him off guard and get him to admit something in the heat of the moment.'

'But how does he manage to do that,' puzzled the Chief. 'You'd have to be some sort of a ventriloquist.'

Making up his mind they'd have to know about it sooner or later, he swallowed. 'If you could get your secretary to fetch my dog, I'll try to explain.'

Addressing the half-asleep pet, Harry said encouragingly, 'Wake up, Prince, tell them about that act we're going to do.'

Protesting, Prince sat up and said, 'I thought you told me not to say anything?'

The effect he produced was dramatic. 'I say, how did he do that? I swear his lips didn't move an inch,' declared Det. Sergeant Matthews. 'That's amazing. Why didn't you tell me about that before?'

'Bless my soul, I didn't know you were one of those trick cyclists,' cried the Chief. 'D'you think he'd fall for it?'

'What a ripping idea,' enthused the Det. Sgt. 'And one of us could be sitting behind him recording it all.'

'You know, it might work, at that,' accepted the Chief

Constable, awestruck. 'I would even come along myself to be there when it all happens, if that can be arranged. What a splendid idea, I'll check my diary. No, dammit, I've got my annual conference coming up. Let me know when they get in touch and I'll see what I can do. Otherwise, you'll have to carry on without me.'

# 13

## SUITABLE FOR THE OCCASION

The call came sooner than expected.

Harry was just getting up next morning when the phone rang unexpectedly, putting him off his stroke as he was shaving and he cut himself, cursing at the interruption. Hastily dabbing at his face he picked up the receiver, wondering who was ringing at this hour.

Glancing at his watch, he frowned. It was still only eight o'clock. 'Hello,' he said cautiously, 'who's that?'

'Alastair Brown here. Sorry to ring so early, but something's cropped up unexpectedly that's affected my plans for putting on that variety act I was talking about.'

'You mean it's cancelled?' asked Harry, detecting a note of anxiety at the other end.

'Good Heavens, no. Nothing like that,' he was assured hastily. 'We can't wait to get it on the road.'

'Then what's the problem?'

'Nothing to worry about. We just wondered whether you'd mind if we were to bring it forward a few days, like, um... tomorrow night.'

Harry turned the suggestion over in his mind. *Why not,* he

thought, *the sooner the better, if we can pull it off.* 'Okay,' he agreed, 'what's the plan?'

He heard a quick sigh of relief at the other end. 'Splendid, I'll let the mayor know. As he sees it, the idea is that there would be a rehearsal in the morning at 9 am and the show itself would be presented as a matinee performance at three in the afternoon.'

Harry was doubtful. 'Are you sure that gives everyone enough time to rehearse?'

'Oh, oodles, so he tells me. I don't suppose you need to do a rehearsal, do you, in your line of business.' He laughed heartily. 'You just have a chat with your dog as you normally do to amuse the audience, and if you find an opportunity you end up by thanking the producer. Am I right?'

'I certainly intend to entertain them,' Harry assured him with conviction, crossing his fingers as he spoke.

'As I thought. The rehearsal's only to make sure the chorus girls get their timing right,' was the satisfied reply. 'I'll ring you back if there's been any last-minute hitch. We're so looking forward to it. Goodbye for now.'

The line went dead and Harry scratched his head thoughtfully. 'I'd better let the others know.'

Checking the time, Harry took a chance and rang the sergeant. As he suspected, there was no reply so he left a message that he was on his way and called for a taxi.

'Sounds as if the mayor's in a panic because the rates are going up,' was the sergeant's verdict, as soon as he heard. 'It couldn't come at a worse time as far as we're concerned. The Chief's away for the weekend, and half my men are on leave.'

'D'you want me to put it off?' asked Harry anxiously.

'No, it might make him suspicious, and we may not get another opportunity like this – we'll just have to go ahead and hope we can pull it off. Whatever happens, I'll be right there with the recorder, so it's all up to you now, Harry. Tell you what, meet me backstage before the curtain goes up and we'll confirm details.'

As the next day dawned, Harry felt a moment of doubt about their makeshift plans, but at the sight of Prince curled up contentedly by the bed he made a conscious effort to reassure himself. *He looks happy enough, let's hope he doesn't forget his lines after our coaching last night.*

Standing in the prompt corner waiting for the sergeant to join him, Harry was about to bend down and stop Prince from getting too restless when he heard an announcement over the loudspeaker requesting Mayor Fox to kindly take over introducing the acts, as the presenter was unavoidably detained.

He peeped through a gap in the curtains and saw the mayor, distinctly annoyed, getting up with some difficulty and making his way to the stage, grumbling all the way. Just then, Harry felt his elbow nudged and Det. Sgt Matthews joined him.

'Quick, there's been a change of plans,' he said. 'Alderman Fox has been asked to take over. He might recognise me from the time I climbed on his balcony. You can't sit behind him now – he'll see what we're up to.'

'But he thinks you're Tom Smith, and you're his prize turn as a ventriloquist. What have you got to worry about?'

Harry decided to come clean, if he was to rely on the backing of his friend if it came to it. With an effort, he tried to explain the true facts about Prince and why he was sworn to secrecy. 'It's no good, it will have to come out, sooner or later. It's not what you think. You're not going to believe this, but Prince isn't a pet dog – he was turned into one by his valet, who fancied himself as a magician.' He turned to see his friend goggling at Prince in amazement. 'I know, I didn't believe it either, when he told me. I'll tell you about it later, when we get a chance. But meanwhile,' he cast a quick look around the hall, 'see if you can grab a box overlooking the stage where nobody will notice you. If anyone tries to enter, you can flash your card at him.'

'You're having me on.'

'I wish I was,' said Harry soberly. 'Let's hope we can make the audience believe it. Here goes, go and grab a seat.'

'Sure you're okay?' The Det. Sgt hesitated, trying to make sense of the extraordinary tale he'd just been told.

'Yes, don't worry about me. Off you go, the place is beginning to fill up.'

After the sergeant left, he moved to the back of the stage where he could safely watch without being seen.

With a great effort, the mayor clambered onto the stage and advanced towards the microphone. He tapped at it and cleared his throat.

'Hrm, ladies and gentlemen, if I can have your attention.' He waited until the chatter died down. 'As you may have gathered, we thought this would be an opportunity to celebrate our good fortune by inviting you all to a special performance we have organised for your entertainment.' As the applause died down, he consulted his notes and waved his arms with a flourish. 'It is therefore with great pleasure that I have been asked to introduce the programme, starting with an opening number by that versatile young dancing group, The High Kickers.'

Judging by their ability to fling their legs up with gay abandon, the troupe were voted a great success and were loudly applauded.

Beaming with pleasure at the way their performance was greeted and the calls for them to continue, The High Kickers finally left the stage, waved farewell by the mayor who was looking forward to the special favours he was expecting later, 'And now,' he glanced hurriedly at his cue sheet, 'I have pleasure in announcing the return of that talented group of acrobats, The High Flyers.'

As his voice droned on extolling the virtues of each act and trying to maintain a mixture of jollity and breeziness, Harry noted that the mayor kept looking at his watch, and was evidently relieved when the lights went up, signalling a break so he could sit down, while a daintily dressed girl appeared down each aisle, selling ice cream.

During the pause, the sergeant joined Harry to compare notes. 'How long have we got?'

'No idea,' admitted Harry. 'I only hope Prince doesn't pass out on me. He's been asleep half the time. Are you okay for sound, where you are?'

'Yes, I've been practising, recording some of the acts. I'll be all right, as long as I can filter out some of the noise from the audience. Look out,' he warned. 'I think the second act's about to start. This where I leave you.'

Refreshed by the break and a quick canoodle with one of the dancing group, Mayor Fox advanced to the front again to introduce what he termed as 'that versatile juggling act, the King Brothers.' This went down well with the audience, and he added his appreciation with a wave. Then, putting on a reverent expression, he followed this up by bowing and piously announcing the presence of, 'that celebrated operatic singer, Susan Paucet' – an introduction that was greeted with polite applause.

As the lofty notes soared higher and higher, some of the younger elements of the audience took the opportunity to sidle out of their seats, ready to make a dash for the exit, only to resume their seats when the last piercing notes mercifully faded away and the lady took her final bow.

'Here, wake up.' Harry shook Prince to get his attention. 'I think this is us.'

'And now, ladies and gentlemen, boys and girls,' beamed

the mayor, 'this is the act I'm sure you've all been waiting for, the one and only Prince, the ventriloquist.' Wiping his face, he returned to his seat, relaxing at the thought it would soon be over.

'Wait a minute,' hooted Prince, waking up on hearing his name mentioned, 'get it right. I'm Prince.' His voice was greeted with gusts of laughter from the audience, thinking it was all part of the act.

'Thank you, Prince,' said Harry, giving him a warning look before taking over, 'I'm sure we'll all be pleased to know that.' He turned to the audience, wondering how to start. The decision was taken for him by one of the more unruly members of the audience seated at the back.

'Tell us about old fatty Fox,' a voice shouted to murmurs of encouragement from some of his mates nearby.

The mayor swivelled around, furious at the interruption, looking in vain for an attendant to evict whoever was responsible.

'Yes, and how he managed to cook the books getting voted,' called another voice, to renewed applause.

Harry gazed out at the sea of faces and gently rebuked the offender with mock solemnity. 'Surely, you are not referring to our esteemed mayor, who has gone to such lengths to put on this splendid entertainment for your benefit?'

'Yes, especially those gorgeous bits of crumpet of his,' added Prince in appreciation.

'They must cost him a bundle,' was the response from a knowing observer in the front row.

'I bet that doesn't go on his expenses,' guessed his companion.

'This is outrageous,' cried the mayor, seeing the situation getting out of hand and praying that someone would come to his rescue. '*Say* something, Smith. Demand an apology.'

I'm sure he didn't mean it,' Harry said soothingly. 'Tell the man, Prince, he'll listen to you.'

'I've never heard anything like it, anyone would think he was on drugs,' said Prince catching on, a remark that provoked a fresh outburst.

'His man charges enough,' accused someone else, looking around for support. 'It costs the earth now.'

'Double what it used to be,' complained another, a remark that had the mayor jumping up and down in a frenzy.

'It's all because of his so-called girlfriends – they started it, putting their rates up,' a lone female voice cried at the back of the hall.

'All because of Gloria,' accused her friend.

'You mean, Lulu.'

'As well as Mimi...'

'And Fifi.'

'I refuse to listen to this anymore,' the mayor howled. 'I'll call my lawyer!'

Sensing they were on the verge of getting at the truth, Prince got the nod and remarked sagely, 'His lawyer, that's a laugh! He'll tell you to own up if he's got any sense.'

'Own up, own up,' some of the audience chanted.

Then another section, in the upper circle, joined in. 'Blame the girls, blame the girls – Gloria, she started it!'

'Don't forget Saucy Sue,' sniggered another, out of spite.

'She wasn't one of that lot,' defended a friend hotly.

'Did someone call?' piped up a fresh voice in the front row, waking up. At the mention of her name, the mayor screamed and fell on his knees. 'Not her as well!' He scrambled to his feet and advanced tottering to the stage, on the verge of giving in.

Up in the gallery, the Det. Sgt gave a thumbs-up and turned on his recorder.

As the mayor reached the microphone to signal his surrender, his former girlfriend, Sue rushed up onto the stage and recognising her old friend, greeted him with delight. 'Harry Bell, I don't believe it. Harry, where have you been lately, are you still in the police? Why didn't you let me know and what have you been up to?'

At the mention of police, the mayor halted in his tracks, the words "I give up!" drying on his lips, unsaid.

'Harry Bell?' he squawked, his old grievances returning, reminding him of their recent encounter on his balcony. 'What the devil do you mean by it, passing yourself off as Tom Smith? You're just a blasted imposter, making those outrageous accusations. Leave this stage immediately and take that confounded ventriloquist dummy with you. I intend to take this up with my lawyer – you haven't heard the last of this, I can promise you.'


'That was a bit of a cock-up,' admitted Harry ruefully later, when Jimmy Matthews returned.

'We practically had it in the bag,' agreed the Det. Sgt, putting his tape recorder away sadly. 'You weren't to know that Saucy Sue would turn up.'

'That's all very well, but what do we do now? We'll just have to wait until the Chief gets back, I suppose,' acknowledged Harry glumly. 'He won't be very pleased when he hears, and meanwhile, I don't fancy asking that inspector, the pompous twit.'

'I know.' Det. Sgt Matthews was struck by a sudden idea. 'Why don't we have a word with Simon Shaw who's in charge of the operation. He was in the SAS, he might have the answer we're looking for.'

'I thought you told me he doesn't like being approached for advice, unless it's an emergency,' said Harry doubtfully.

'What d'you call this, if not an emergency?'

Ringing Simon Shaw's office somewhat reluctantly, Harry was put through and after briefly explaining the situation he was invited to join the man right away with the Det. Sgt and discuss the matter.

'As soon as I can. I have to leave Prince, my dog, with someone,' he explained apologetically.

'Bring him with you,' Shaw instructed. 'I have another appointment shortly and we don't want to waste time.'

Tucking Prince under his arm, Harry and his friend set out to walk the short distance to the office and got there just as Simon's secretary was packing up, ready to leave.

'Ah, there you are.' Simon Shaw got up to greet them. 'My secretary has informed me that my next appointment has been cancelled, so I have some more time on my hands, after all. I suggest we hold our meeting at my private conference office just down the road.'

Reaching their destination, he cautioned, 'I have just been advised by security that my office has been bugged, which is the reason I have suggested holding our meeting here, where we will not be overheard.'

Having explained the situation, he invited them to take a seat around an oval table while he reminded them of the position to date.

'So, as I understand it, the Chief Constable and Inspector Pain were both aware of your plans to persuade the mayor to make a public confession of his involvement in the drugs trade.'

'Yes,' confirmed Harry. 'We needed proof, so the Chief left it to us to get him to confess, as part of my act.'

'But it didn't succeed, I take it?'

As Harry hesitated, the Det. Sgt broke in to cover his embarrassment. 'No, it wasn't Harry's fault, though. The mayor was on the point of admitting it when one of his former girlfriends recognised Harry and gave the game away.' He added, 'There was a lot of heckling going on from the audience, but when he realised he had nothing to fear, he changed tack and threatened to contact his solicitors.'

'Let's get it clear.' Shaw directed his attention to the Det. Sergeant. 'Were you prepared to accept his admission if it was given in front of the audience, acting as witnesses?'

'Not exactly,' admitted the other. 'I had a tape recorder ready to confirm anything he said.'

'I see, a wise precaution. In that case, perhaps you would hand it over and I'll see that nobody tampers with it. Don't worry, I'll look after it.'

As he placed it safely out of sight in a drawer, Harry felt in his bones that something was wrong with Simon Shaw's view of the situation, but he couldn't put a finger on it.

With a broad smile, Shaw remarked cheerfully, 'Now that has been established, we can relax while we decide on our next course of action. Tom... I mean Harry of course, I forgot, why don't you fetch a bottle and some glasses from the kitchen, to help us sort our ideas out. It's been a long day, and I'm sure we could all do with a drink.'

Getting up to do as he was bid, Harry wondered how long Shaw had called him 'Harry', if he ever had, but kept the thought to himself. Once in the kitchen he found a tray already prepared, and as he picked it up he accidentally knocked over a small picture frame that came apart, revealing several family photographs stuck together. Hurriedly replacing them, his eye caught a glimpse of an elderly man in one of them, wearing a uniform, displaying what looked like... yes it was, a swastika! He looked more closely to make sure. There was no doubt about it, and the face was the spitting image of Simon Shaw.

No, it couldn't be, the man was grey-haired, perhaps a relative? No time to investigate now, it would have to wait until later. He stuffed it in his pocket and replaced the other photos, setting the picture frame back in its place.

His head was spinning. If it *was* him, how did they let him enlist in the SAS? Perhaps he fooled them, no, that would not have been possible. Wait a minute, perhaps he was something similar, not the SAS, but that was crazy, how would he have got away with it?

Answering an impatient cry from the other room, he quickly picked up the tray and carried it in, apologising as he did so. 'Sorry, not sure which bottle you meant.'

'Never mind, sit down, I'll see to it,' replied Shaw affably. 'I'm sure I can find something suitable for the occasion.'

As soon as the door closed behind him, Harry got up and started pulling at some of the drawers.

'Ah, here we are.' He fished out the miniature recorder and handed it over. 'Quick, set it to record. Don't ask, just do it, Jimmy, before he comes back.'

Puzzled, the Det. Sgt set it in motion and placed it on the seat next to him, out of sight.

A few minutes later the door opened again, revealing their host brandishing a bottle. 'Here we are, just what I was looking for, try this.' He poured out two glasses with his back to them, before handing them over. 'Cheers.'

Leaving his glass untouched, Harry asked pointedly, 'There seems to be one missing, where's yours?'

Simon laughed breezily. 'Silly me, here goes.'

He quickly half-filled another glass and held it up, crying 'Slainte' before drinking.

Out of politeness, Harry and the Det. Sgt cautiously sipped their glasses before putting them down again.

'Not a bad year,' said Simon passing judgement. Tipping his glass up, he encouraged them saying, 'Come on, drink up, don't waste it.'

'I'd rather like to hear your views on the situation I mentioned first,' said Harry persuasively. 'After your service in the SAS, you must be used to making a quick assessment.'

'True,' replied Simon modestly. 'We had some pretty tough decisions to make at times, it wasn't all that easy.'

'Like having your picture taken when you were in the SS?'

said Harry casually, holding up the photo he'd discovered.

Shaw spluttered over his drink, and recovering replied lightly, 'Where on earth did you find that? It was... when we had a fancy dress party one year. Grandad Shaw had us all fooled.'

Seeing their glasses untouched, he threw the contents into the nearest pot plant. 'Forget about the wine, what about a malt whiskey, I can vouch for that.' He filled up another glass and emptied it with a flourish to show there was nothing wrong with it. 'Here you are, try one.'

Harry hesitated, then reassured that it came from the same bottle, lifted his glass in a toast and the Det. Sgt followed.

'That's better,' their host said, smacking his lips. 'Have another.' He held up the bottle invitingly.

Harry had to admit that the whiskey tasted as good as his host had promised. Despite his initial suspicions, he felt he needed it after all his wasted efforts in trying to unmask the mayor, and the Det. Sgt agreed. Once that was dispatched, another two glasses followed in quick succession without any objection.

Suffice it to say, that after a few more follow-ups Shaw had no difficulty in slipping a tablet in their drinks without being observed.

Making sure that the dose had taken effect, he bent over and prodded them, calling out loudly, 'Right then, what's next on the agenda?'

His words made no impression on his audience, they were both lying flat out, but it was enough to wake up the dog who had been happily dozing behind a nearby sofa.

'Prince wants to do wee-wees.'

Luckily, his demands largely went unnoticed with all the snoring that was going on, but tripping over the dog a moment later, Shaw misheard and thought it must have come from Harry, so he led Prince out to do what was needed.

Emerging from his half-drugged state, Harry yawned and tried to stretch, but found he was powerless and unable to move. 'Jimmy,' he managed, 'I don't seem to be able to feel anything.'

'Me neither,' complained the Det. Sgt, making an effort. 'Wonder what's happened.'

'It must have been the drink,' decided Harry, 'but I didn't see him do it.'

'You were too far gone, that's why,' explained their host, looming over them, all traces of his earlier charm replaced by one of gloating triumph.

Harry groaned. 'I shouldn't have fallen for that tale about the photo. So you were in the SS, after all.'

'No, you were wrong there,' he was corrected sharply. 'That was a picture of my grandfather.'

Seeing that he had nothing more to fear, he went on, 'You wouldn't understand, his real name was Hans Shafunbach, an Oberfuhrer in the SS.' As he announced the title, he sprang stiffly to attention and saluted. 'He died fighting for our glorious fatherland in the last stages of the war, and it has been my one aim in life to follow in his footsteps and complete his mission.'

After a pause, the fanatical gleam died out of his voice and he continued in a matter-of-fact tone, 'My father wisely changed our name, and I adopted the identity of a friend in the SAS who was killed in a family car crash in order to gain the necessary battle experience. Not that any of this will be of use to you,' he added with grim satisfaction. 'Now that you know the truth, you have signed your own death warrants and you will shortly trouble us no more.'

To play for time, knowing their conversation was being recorded, Harry prompted him. 'What made you join your PR company?'

The fanatical gleam was back in his eyes. 'To make money, of course, to build up a fighting fund for a new fatherland!'

'Of course,' soothed Harry, thinking the man had completely gone off his rocker and was barking mad. 'What stopped you, was it Trustworthy?'

'That conniving rat,' was the scornful reply. 'He wanted fifty percent of the profits, some hope. He wasn't content with taking over that B&B business to keep in with the mayor for a price, the moron. He got what was coming to him, like all the others who dared to complain. That stupid secretary of his didn't even recognise his body after all the trouble I'd taken, just because he wasn't wearing his favourite shoes.'

'And Mayor Fox, is he one of yours?'

'That greedy pig. He ruined it all by spending the money we made from drugs on those tarts of his, instead of investing in my plans for creating a new fatherland, as I instructed. Do not worry, my friend, Scarface has told me all about it. I'll see that Fox gets his reward, after I've dealt with you, you interfering amateurs.'

'You'll never get away with it,' gritted the Det. Sgt, attempting to get up and falling back helplessly.

'Don't worry, I'll fix you too, you miserable copper.'

'You and who else?' interrupted Prince, sitting up.

Shaw sneered. 'And don't think those ventriloquist tricks of yours will help you either. I've got a little time bomb here that will take care of you, and nobody will be any the wiser.'

'That's what you think,' said Prince, advancing bravely, ready to attack his ankle.

'No, don't try it,' entreated Harry helplessly, unable to move. 'Stay where you are.'

Ignoring the threat, Shaw reached for his suitcase and lifting out a clocklike device, started to wind it up before setting the hands. Hearing a car toot, he exclaimed, 'Ah, that sounds like Scarface now, let me see, ten minutes, that should do the trick. Out of the way, scum.' He aimed a kick at the dog as he headed for the door, sending Prince sprawling and leaving him in a dazed and winded state.

Before departure, Shaw propped the clock up on the window ledge and waving a farewell, slammed the door behind him.

As soon as he had gone, Harry yelled at the dog frantically, trying to gain his attention. 'Wake up, Prince, mind that clock.' Fearing his last hope of seeing his beloved Sheila again was vanishing by the second, he redoubled his efforts.

'PRINCE, wake up!'

'W-what's that?' The animal stirred. 'Did someone call?'

'Yes!' shrieked Harry and Jimmy in unison. 'It's that clock – mind what you do with it – it's dynamite!'

'What d'you mean, dynamite?'

'Don't touch it, untie us so we can throw it out of the window, it's due to go off any minute. It's a bomb!'

Prince lurched to his feet and staggering towards the window, gazed up forlornly. 'I feel all wobbly.'

'Don't argue, come and untie us, otherwise we've had it.'

Prince shook his head to clear it. 'I don't think I c-can manage it. I haven't eaten all day – I haven't got the strength.'

'Do that, and I'll give you the biggest slap-up spread you've ever had,' promised Harry wildly.

That did it. Without thinking about his own safety, Prince made a frantic lunge and gripping the cord attached to the clock between his teeth he swung it at the window with all his remaining energy. The glass splintered and the clock disappeared through the gap and fell below, landing in the back of the waiting car.

A few minutes later there was a blinding flash, followed by an almighty roar and the window and half the wall collapsed, sending fragments flying and catching Harry a glancing blow, knocking him out.

## 14

## DOCTOR'S ORDERS

When he came to, all he was aware of was the gentle touch of fingers smoothing his brow and an anxious face peering down at him. Then the mists cleared.

'Sheila,' he whispered, and as he reached up for her hand, a stabbing pain made him gasp. 'Ouch.'

'No, don't try to move, darling, doctor's orders.'

'Did you say, "darling"?' he croaked.

For an answer, she kissed his hand and placed it back lovingly under the sheet. 'Will you forgive me for all those horrid things I said to you? Must go, the nurse only allowed me a few minutes, just to see if you're all right. See you soon.' She blew him a kiss, and waving a hand disappeared from view.

Harry sank back, re-living every blissful moment, and savouring her words drifted off to sleep.

Some hours later, a nurse tiptoed in and seeing him stir and open his eyes, whispered, 'You have another visitor, if you're up to it, love. A Det. Sgt, so he says.'

Harry propped himself up awkwardly while she checked his pulse and temperature.

Satisfied, the nurse called out, 'You can see him now for a

short while, sir. Make sure you don't over excite him, he's still recovering.'

Det. Sgt Matthews hobbled in with the aid of a stick, his head heavily bandaged.

'Can't stay long, doctor's orders,' he reported with a grin. 'Just thought you'd like to hear the latest.'

'Take a pew,' offered Harry, waving at the nearest seat. 'Look's as if you've copped it, as well.'

'Thanks.' His friend lowered himself down gingerly. 'Chief's been on at me, he said we should have checked that nutter out properly in the first place.' He sighed ruefully. 'He was right, he had us all fooled, except you, of course. Good thing you tipped me off about that photo. Still, we've got the proof he wanted, even though it wasn't the one he expected.'

'I wasn't all that sure myself,' admitted Harry. 'Never mind that, don't keep me keep me in suspense,' he urged. 'What happened when the bomb went off, did he get away?'

'You're joking, he caught it good and proper. Not much left of him. Still, it saved us a trial and any awkward questions about what he was up to,' allowed the Det. Sergeant. 'The same goes for Scarface, thank goodness. We won't see him again. He would have been in for a hefty sentence had he survived, if I'm any judge, and so will old Foxy, unless his solicitor turns out to be a magician.'

'Oh, my goodness, how is Prince?' Harry caught his arm at the mention of the word magician. 'Is he all right?'

'He's fine, he managed to miss the blast, luckily for him. He's waiting for that slap-up treat you were promising him. That reminds me, I'm told there's a reward out for those villains – which should come to a tidy sum, I guess.' He counted out on his fingers. 'There's Trustworthy, who we now know as Ernest Banks, our late con artist; Scarface Willie, drug dealer; and the king pin himself, Simon Shaw, whose prints match those of Butch Jones on that leaflet, a self-confessed anarchist and Lord knows what else.'

'Is that who he was, Butch Jones? Wait a minute,' said Harry, thinking it over. 'If there's any reward to come out of this, it should go to Prince. He saved our lives, don't forget.'

'Don't worry, I'll see to that,' promised the Det. Sgt. 'The lucky dog... sorry, my mistake – I should have said, your friend, Prince.'

Looking for words of comfort, he added hastily before Harry nodded off again, 'Now you're on the mend, I gather you are being shipped off to your B&B where your friends are waiting to look after you.'

And so it proved. The first sign that made him aware he was back in familiar surroundings as he came to was the kindly face of Jazz bending over him.

'Sorry to disturb you, sir. I thought you might like to know about the latest situation regarding his Highness.'

'His Highness? You mean Prince – what situation?'

'Bearing in mind your warm appreciation of my master's recent successful intervention on your behalf without regard to his own personal safety, I decided that perhaps the time had come to reward him for his efforts.'

Harry heaved himself up and made an effort to follow what was going on. 'What's this all about? And what's Mrs M doing there behind you, grinning all over her face? I haven't forgotten about that spread I promised him.'

Jazz stepped back respectfully. 'If you would both care to step this way, sir, I will endeavour to explain.'

Mystified, Harry got up, and slipping on his dressing gown followed Jazz, Mrs M hanging on to his arm, beaming.

'What's this all about?' he asked, bewildered.

'Shush, it's a surprise,' she whispered.

They came to a halt outside the guest bedroom where Sheila joined them, putting a finger to her lips.

'What is going on?' insisted Harry.

Instead of answering, Jazz tapped on the door discreetly. 'May we be permitted to enter, your Highness?'

Instead of Prince's piping yelp, they heard a happy girlish laugh. 'Of course.'

Opening the door with a flourish, Jazz stood to one side and ushered them in.

All they could make out was the sight of Mary bending over a muffled figure hidden under what looked like Prince's rug taken from his basket.

'Good Lord, you don't mean what I think you mean?' stammered Harry, shaken.

Half giggling and absurdly happy, Mary whipped the rug away, disclosing a sight that made them catch their breath.

It was Prince, no longer in the shape of his faithful pet, but a handsome and dashing Prince, attired in a resplendent uniform.

In the awed silence that followed, Harry did not notice Mrs M had slipped away. Before he could think of what to say, she reappeared bearing a loaded tray of drinks which she deposited with a whoop on the nearest table.

Seizing a glass, Prince held it up in a toast. 'To the sweetest, most wonderful girl in the world – Mary, my own love.' To prove it, he gathered her in his arms, leaving her blushing and half protesting at the sudden attention.

'I proposed to her this morning and to my astonishment she said "yes". I still can't believe it.'

'It's magic, oh, my dear, I'm so happy for you.' Mrs M rushed forward and hugged her, amid a chorus of good wishes and congratulations. 'Tell me all about it.'

Mary glanced up at Prince and confessed. 'I always felt there was something there I could love, directly I held him in my arms, when that silly sergeant tried to arrest me.'

Seeing the baffled looks on the faces around him, Harry

waved Jazz forward to explain the whole story from the beginning.

'I knew he was a magician directly he appeared at the door and made everything look so different somehow,' said Mrs M at the finish. 'Tell me, dear, what are your plans for the future?'

Mary turned shyly to Prince for guidance.

Prince came to attention and bowed. 'We will return to Palmesia as soon as it can be arranged and celebrate with a state banquet and wedding fit for a king, or should I say, as Prince Henry, which is my name.' He smiled and drew her to him. 'There will be rejoicing throughout the land to mark the occasion.'

'Is this true?' Harry took Mary aside, astonished at the sudden turn of events. 'But how do you know he'll be able to? I thought his cousin was in charge of the country. Will they accept him?'

'I don't care either way,' she answered simply. 'I love Henry, not his silly old country.' She turned and faced her beloved, kissing him devotedly. 'Whatever happens, we're together now, that's all I care about.'

'There now.' Sheila nudged Harry. 'Why can't you say something romantic like that?'

Before he could assure her of his devotion, Prince Henry overheard and intervened. 'It's not as bad as Mary makes out,' he reassured them. 'I hear from my friends in Palmesia that they can't wait to get rid of my cousin. He's ruining the country. All I need is a band of trusty friends I can rely on to fill up some of the important posts I have in mind, before I return and take over.'

He nodded at his friend encouragingly, but Harry ignored the hint. He was still uncertain of his own circumstances and refused to be drawn, despite the tempting suggestion.

At the first opportunity, he discussed the situation frankly with Sheila.

'Darling, I know we've had our ups and downs, but I really do love you with all my heart and always will, but...'

'Did you say you love me? Why didn't you say so, you silly. Kiss me.' Before he could utter another word, she threw herself in his arms and began to smother him with kisses.

After a satisfying embrace, he reluctantly eased her away and confessed, 'You do realise, I've not much to offer you, apart from what little savings I've made from my undercover work, and that's all finished now.'

Her answer was swift and to the point. 'I don't care. What about Mary, she doesn't mind what the future brings.'

Harry took a deep breath and came to a decision. 'You're absolutely right, I'll have a word with Jim and see what he has to say.'

But Jim Matthews was discouraging. 'You haven't heard the latest. The Chief's just been offered a new post under his cousin on the admin side at Scotland Yard. He's over the moon about it. They're all after his job now, especially that pain in the neck Chief Inspector. He's making sure everyone knows about it, too, throwing his weight around and hoping he'll be left in charge. They're all keeping their heads down in case they put a foot wrong.'

'There goes my chance of any work then,' admitted Harry. 'He's always been jealous of me, I can't understand why.'

'Don't worry,' you're not the only one,' consoled the Det. Sergeant. 'He's the same with anyone he thinks is likely to get in his way.'

Having crossed that possibility off his list, Harry picked up the phone to see if Prince Henry was still serious about his offer, and getting no response decided to ring the Earl to find out how Geoffrey, his grandson, was getting on with his treatment. Instead of the Earl, the call was answered by Manners, his valet.

'I'm afraid the master is out just now,' he was informed.

Then recognising the voice, Manners was quite apologetic. 'I must apologise, sir, everything is rather topsy-turvy at the moment, ever since the master took over the hotel. The mayor decided he had some urgent business that required his presence overseas. It was all rather unexpected.' Explaining what had happened, he went on, 'You may not have heard, sir. He received the offer at rather short notice to take over the hotel after the sudden departure of Mayor Fox and we have been rather stretched getting back to normal, sir. Before I forget, the master was most anxious to get in touch with you.'

Not wishing to add to the Earl's problems and assured by Manners that Geoffrey was on the mend, Harry asked to be remembered and promised to get in touch again as soon as he had sorted out his own immediate and more pressing problems.

After turning it over in his mind and discussing the alternatives on offer with Sheila and getting her agreement, Harry went in search of Prince Henry to say he was available, if the offer was still open. Confirming the arrangement with Sheila, he added on the spur of the moment, 'Why don't you persuade your mother to come with us? I'm sure we can find her something to do when we get out there.' Heartened by her enthusiastic response he left her to pack, and calling a taxi made his way to Police HQ to let his friend know about the outcome.

Hoping the Det. Sgt would join him in his new venture, he was disappointed to learn that Jim was looking after his parents after a recent car accident so it would be a family decision after all, just him and Sheila, together with her mother. Finally, the last port of call was the Chief Constable who he anticipated would be full of his plans for the future.

Much to his surprise, Colonel Slaughter appeared to be more put out by the upset his own imminent departure might cause than anything else. 'Allow that idiot Pain to take over while they're choosing the next Chief Constable? Over my dead body. The man's a disaster, what can we do to stop it? Come on, Harry, you are usually full of ideas, even though that last ventriloquist act of yours didn't come off.'

Floored by the unexpected appeal, Harry floundered. 'To be honest,' he admitted, 'I'm so confused about what sort of post they expect me to take up in Palmesia, I wouldn't know what to suggest. They even thought I might be interested in taking on the post as Director of Entertainment. I've already explained that I'm not a ventriloquist, that was just a ruse to get the mayor to confess.'

'Knowing our Chief Inspector,' interrupted Jim jokingly, 'I don't suppose he would mind what the title was, as long as the salary was right.'

'That's it!' broke in Colonel Slaughter. 'Leave it to me. I'll have a word with him.'

'Steady on,' cautioned Harry. 'I'm not sure we should use that as an inducement.'

'You're quite right,' agreed the Chief Constable. 'Let's just say that by the time I've finished with him, he'll think he's head of Scotland Yard and they're lucky to get him.'

Meanwhile, when the news filtered down the grapevine about the mayor's disappearance, his former girlfriends began to appreciate how dependent they had become in accepting his handouts, despite all the complaints they had made in the past.

Calling a meeting, the girls read reports about the unrest in Palmesia and the opportunities that were opening up to encourage and welcome the return of tourists and were impressed.

'What say, girls?' cried Gloria. 'Looks like the opportunity we've been waiting for. What about trying our luck? I'm flat broke after trusting that scum of a boyfriend of mine to invest all my savings in his rubbishy schemes. It says here the place is oozing with new cabarets and dance shows. It's got our name on it. Hands up all those willing to give it a chance.'

Gratified by the response, Gloria started cutting out the details in the newspaper. 'This is the opportunity I've been waiting for after that rat Arthur scarpered with all my money. Right, pack your bags, girls. Palmesia, here we come!'

Relieved that the Chief had promised to get the threat of the inspector off his friend's back, Harry turned up at the docks with Sheila and her mother, complete with baggage, ready to embrace his new life.

In an attempt to soothe her mother at the thought of leaving her B&B business behind and to stifle her own doubts, Sheila did her best to look on the bright side. 'Now don't forget, Mum, that nice housekeeper of ours will be there as well with Prince Henry, so we won't be alone. He'll probably be full of ideas, knowing Jazz.'

'That's all very well, but he'll have his time taken up looking after his master. And how do we know Prince Henry will be able to find a job for young Harry with that cousin lurking in the background?'

'I'm sure he'll find something,' attempted Harry, anxious to calm them down, his words almost lost in the exchanges.

In the midst of the heated debate that was developing, nobody noticed a familiar figure bearing down on them.

They were so engrossed in their argument that the greeting shout of "Harry!" made no immediate impression. It wasn't until he looked up in search of something that would offer a diversion that he realised who it was.

'William! I mean, sir. How are you?'

'Harry! Thank heavens, I've caught you in time. I thought I'd missed you.'

'That's very good of you to come and see us off,' said Harry awkwardly, putting down his suitcase and holding out a hand. 'Is Geoffrey all right?'

'Never mind about Geoffrey,' said the Earl impatiently, 'he's fine. Look, forget about that ferry, Manners has been making enquiries and heard where you're going. I've only just found out. Don't go, I implore you.'

'But why?' Harry said blankly.

'Because I want you to stay... with me.'

Before Harry could utter a word, the Earl blurted out, 'I've been going over the whole business, over and over again. I was so taken aback by your news about Lady M and your connection when you mentioned it, I didn't stop to work it out.' He pressed Harry's hand. 'Now that I've had time to think about it and realise what a sacrifice your family must have made over the years, I've realised what an idiot I was to let you go. Will you ever forgive me?'

'Of course,' responded Harry automatically. He reflected, 'I expect my grandad would have been pleased to know that, it would have put his mind to rest. It all seems a long time ago now.' He released his grip reluctantly. 'I have to go, though. You don't realise, I've been offered a new job abroad now that I've given up working for the police.'

'Forget about that, come and work for me,' implored the Earl. 'I need someone to take over running the hotel for me and I immediately thought of you. You'd have a free hand, just say the word.'

'I'd love to,' admitted Harry ruefully, 'but I've already promised to take on this other post.' He added after a sudden thought, 'And I've just remembered. I need to find something for Sheila's mother to do, now that she's given up her B&B business.'

'No problem, she can run the restaurant in the hotel and take in paying guests at the same time.'

Stunned by the offer, Harry was vaguely aware of Sheila clutching his arm and whispering eagerly in his ear, 'Tell him "Yes", you idiot.'

'I think the general consensus is that we would be most grateful,' acknowledged Harry weakly, at the thought of what it would mean to their lives.

'Now that has been settled,' declared the Earl with satisfaction, 'I can make it official by adopting you as a member of my family – I know Geoffrey will be delighted.'

Overcome by the sudden and unexpected offer, Harry couldn't take it in. He collapsed and had to be helped to the nearest seat to help him recover. In the confusion, he bumped into the next arrival, nearly knocking him over.

Straightening up and brushing away any imaginary dust specks that might spoil his smart new Bond Street suit after the unexpected encounter, Chief Inspector Pain marched up the gangplank and addressed the nearest seaman in his usual overbearing manner. 'Inform the Captain that the New Director of Entertainment for Palmesia is on board. Don't waste my time, get a move on and do as I say. See that my luggage is taken below – first class, of course.'

There was a flurry of excitement as the news spread throughout the ferry. 'Did you hear that, girls?' crowed Gloria. 'Now's our opportunity to get signed up for one of the shows. After him!'

Headed by Gloria, they chased after their quarry, finally running him to earth, and face to face, she flung out an arm and pointed dramatically. 'I don't believe it, this must be my lucky day.' She advanced menacingly. 'What have you got to say for yourself? Take a good look at him, girls, it's Arthur, my ex-boyfriend. Where's my money, you thieving rat?'

Cornered, Inspector Pain croaked, 'There must be a mistake, madam, I assure you. You must be mistaking me for someone else.'

Pressing him against the rail, Gloria snorted scornfully. 'You bet there is, Arthur. The mistake you made was thinking you could get away with it. Where's my savings? I'll count up to three. One, two and... stop him!'

With a last desperate look around and seeing the game was up, the hunted man gulped and vaulted over the rail to be lost to view in the swirling wake.

'Lower the lifeboat,' thundered Gloria. 'If he thinks he's got away with it, he'd better think again.'

END

*This book is dedicated to the memory of P.G. Wodehouse*